I0538182

FALLING FOR THE TRAINER

Heart-Warming Mature Romance. Set in the Exciting World of Horse Racing.

ELSIE AND BELLA SERIES - BOOK 2
Book 2

DEE GIBSON

GIBSON PUBLISHING

Chapter 1

The rich aroma of smoky bacon and fresh coffee was in the air, as Bella stepped through the wide glass doors of the sprawling Federation house. Sunlight spilled across the patio, illuminating a scene transformed overnight. Yesterday round tables covered in crisp white linen and extravagant floral centrepieces had been, now long wooden tables stretched beneath the morning sky. The wedding flowers settled onto the long wooden tables.

Beyond the glistening pool, a stand of ghost gums swayed gently, their silver branches framing the endless view of the green valleys beyond. Steve had married Elsie in this glorious setting yesterday. Guests, now in relaxed attire, murmured over hearty plates of breakfast. The occasional burst of laughter mixed with the clatter of cutlery. Bella took in the amazing view of the stud farm.

A broad-smiling cook gestured toward a side table. 'Coffee and orange juice over there, food's right here. What'll it be?'

'It looks so different out here today,' Bella mused,

reaching for a plate. 'Yep, magic happens overnight,' the cook chuckled. 'Scrambled eggs and crispy bacon, please.' As the cook piled food onto her plate, he asked, 'Did you have fun at the wedding yesterday?' 'I did,' Bella said, grinning. 'It was beautiful. My feet are reminding me I danced way too long, though.' They laughed together as Bella turned to find a seat. She settled in at a table where conversation buzzed with wedding reminiscences.

'Here's the bridesmaid,' said a guest. 'You looked gorgeous yesterday Bella. 'Where'd you get your dress?' Bella smiled. 'Thanks, I found it on Puckle Street in Moonee Ponds, some great little boutiques there.'

'Did Elsie find hers there too?'

'Yep, we went together,

'Yes it was.' Bella agreed The memory of silk against her skin and the scent of her bouquet flickering through her mind. The setting had been perfect. Her gaze drifted toward the paddocks. Horses. She'd always noticed them, always felt drawn to them. Even loved photos of them. Two horses played in the distance, their coats gleaming in the sun. Growing up in the city, she'd dreamed of having a horse of her own, but it had remained just that—a dream.

Michael dropped into the seat beside her, his plate overloaded. Bella smirked. 'You plan on eating all that, Mick?' His brows shot up, he grinned. 'I'll do it proud.'

'Still a growing lad,' Bill teased. She and Elsie teased Michael relentlessly, shortening his name which he hated. Michael was in his forties and the manager of the lifestyle village where Elsie and Bella lived. He was the chauffeur for the bride and bridesmaid yesterday. Driving them up from Melbourne. Laughter rippled through the table. Conversations wove in and out, recollections of the wedding sparking more laughter. 'Elsie and Steve took forever to leave on their honeymoon,' someone said, stretching with a yawn.

'Probably having too much fun,' Michael added. The thought of Elsie already halfway to Italy sent a pang through Bella. Just a few hours apart, and she already missed her best friend. 'This place is breathtaking,' she murmured, taking in the view. Michael nodded. 'Doesn't matter what the weather is, this place always looks magnificent.' 'How about we head back to Melbourne around eleven-thirty?' he suggested.

'Sounds good, as long as I have time for a walk to see the horses first.' Bill straightened his hat. 'I'll show you around.'

'Thank you Bill, that will be lovely.'

Leo appeared, coffee in hand, and took the seat opposite Bella. His easy smile lingered a little longer than necessary, his deep-set brown eyes unreadable. She found herself remembering the way he had spun her around the dance floor last night, his strong hands guiding her effortlessly. 'That band was fantastic,' she said. 'Are they local?'

'Nah, we bring them in from Melbourne. They can play anything.' Bella grinned. 'Wasn't it a great night?' Leo chuckled.

'You're quite the dancer, Bella.'

'Oh, I loved it. My feet, not so much. Sneakers today.' Leo lifted his coffee, eyes still on her. 'How are you getting back to Melbourne?' 'Michael's driving. He's giving me time to visit the horses before we leave.

'I'd love to show you our stud farm.' Bill raised a brow. 'I already volunteered.' Leo smirked. 'You can come too, Bill.' Michael swallowed a mouthful of bacon. 'I'll tag along after I finish this feast.'

Bill rose, stretching. 'Anyone up for meeting the horses?'

Bella followed the group through the house paddock gate. The scent of fresh grass filled the air as two horses grazed nearby. Her breath caught. One of them—majestic and powerful stood apart. 'Is that Danger Man? Bella gushed.

'Yes that's Danger Man,' Bill said. 'Independent personality, that one.'

'Will he let us pat him?' Bella asked.

'Leo will bring him over.'

'We bet on him in The Melbourne Cup, and we won nearly five grand.'

'Yes, he was the winner alight.' Bill said proudly. Leo's phone buzzed. He ignored it. Then it buzzed again. A muscle in his jaw tightened. He pulled it out, glanced at the screen, and shut it off with a flick of his thumb. Bella had walked straight up to Danger Man, without fear. Leo's sharp voice cracked the air. 'Hey! What the hell are you giving him?'

Bella jerked back, startled. 'An apple from the kitchen. I thought all horses loved apples.' Leo stalked toward her, eyes flashing. 'Not all horses are Melbourne Cup winners. Pays to ask first.' Before he could snatch it away, Danger Man had already taken the apple, crunching it happily.

Bella bit her lip, resisting the urge to roll her eyes. She continued stroking his sleek coat, feeling the warmth of his breath against her skin. The horse nudged into her shoulder. 'He wants another apple,' Leo muttered. Bella laughed. 'No, he loves me.'

'Nah, just wants more apple.' Bill chuckled. 'Looks like he's taken a liking to Bella. You good with horses?'

Bella shook her head. 'No, always wanted one, but I'm a city girl.' Bill nodded. 'You're a natural, especially with Danger Man. Wouldn't you say, Leo? Leo shrugged, his response clipped. 'It's the apple.'

Bella ignored his tone. 'Do we have time to see Velvet Glow? I saw her first race in Bendigo.' Leo's gaze sharpened, a flicker of something unreadable passing through his eyes. 'Oh, did you?' 'Yes, Steve took Elsie and me. She came fourth. I helped get her ready it was the best day.' Leo exhaled, his voice flat. 'She's in the outer paddocks with the young horses.

'Not easy to get to.' Bill said. 'Best leave it. Steve's got a trainer keeping an eye on her.' Bella smiled at Bill. 'That's okay.'

As they headed back, Bella snapped more photos of the landscape, of Danger Man, of Bill. But not Leo. He trailed behind, silent, his posture stiff. A heavy stillness clung to him, and the tension in his shoulders was unmistakable. His easy charm from earlier had evaporated, replaced by something distant and brooding. Leo barely heard the idle chatter around him. His thoughts swirled with the weight of the phone calls. He had recognised the number the second it flashed across the screen, his ex-wife. Again. He had let it ring the first time, hoping she'd get the hint. But she never did. The second time, irritation had prickled at the edge of his patience. By the third, he'd answered, jaw tight, already knowing what was coming. 'Leo, my car won't start. I need you to come over. I am at my sister Janets.' It was never a request. Always a demand. Always an expectation. His fists clenched at the memory of her tone, the way she still acted as if he were on call for her every inconvenience. He wasn't her husband anymore, yet somehow, she never quite let him go. She always found a way to reel him back in one excuse after another.

'I've already said no. Don't call again,' he'd snapped before ending the call with more force than necessary. But even now, it lingered. The tight knot in his stomach, the feeling of being pulled back into something he thought he had left behind. He walked slower than the others, boot scuffing against tufts of taller grass, his mind heavy with the push and pull of old habits, of a past that refused to stay buried. Bill, up ahead, glanced back. 'You coming, son?' Leo forced a nod, picking up his pace, but the weight in his chest remained. The crisp morning air did nothing to clear the tension in his head. The sight of Bella, laughing lightly at something Bill said, should have been enough to ground him back into the present. Instead, it only made him more aware of the storm brewing inside him. The easy mood of the morning had shifted. And for the first time that day, Leo wished he were anywhere else but here.

Chapter 2

As the stud farm receded into the distance, Bella rested her cheek against the cool glass of the car side window, watching the landscape shift with every turn. The winding mountain road revealed glimpses of the valley below, a patchwork of sprawling mansions and manicured gardens. Swimming pools sparkled in the sunlight like scattered jewels, so pristine they looked surreal.

'Look at that house,' she murmured, wonder slipping into her voice. 'And that swimming pool it's massive.' Michael chuckled, keeping his attention on the road.

'Humongous, alright. Though I doubt it gets much use up here in the chill.' Bella's thoughts drifted away from the scenery, back to the memory of Danger Man. She could still feel the warmth of his breath, the way his sleek coat gleamed under the morning sun, the intensity of his gaze as he leaned into her touch. She spoke softly, almost to herself. 'Isn't Danger Man magnificent?'

Michael nodded. 'He is. Not every day you meet a Melbourne Cup winner. The pride they have in him is something else.' Bella smiled though her tone sharpened. 'Leo's pride is something else too. He's such a stickler for routine, isn't he?' Michael laughed.

'Oh, he's not so bad. I'd say he's got a soft spot for you.' She let out a huff, crossing her arms.

'I'd rather he didn't, snapping at me over one apple who needs that kind of drama?'

'Guess he'd have driven you home if you'd let him,' Michael teased. Bella turned, her brows knitting into a frown. 'Absolutely not. He practically bit my head off. Is he always that uptight?' Michael shrugged, a knowing smirk tugging at his lips.

'Not really. Leo just... cares a lot about the horses.' Bella rolled her eyes, the memory of his scowl flashing through her mind. Beneath the charm he'd shown as her partner at the wedding was a streak of something colder, more rigid. 'If he's this intense over an apple, pity his wife if she ever leaves something out of place.' Michael's laugh filled the car.

'No wife he's single. Just him and the horses to keep things tidy.' 'Figures,' Bella muttered. 'Usually, I get along fine with horse people, but he turned into a grump today.'

Michael chuckled again, clearly amused. Bella, however, found her irritation lingering. She pressed her lips together, the faint hum of the tires against the road filling the silence. 'As if I'd harm a horse,' she murmured, more to herself than to Michael. 'That doesn't excuse being so rude.' The image of Leo's disapproving glare refused to leave her mind, stark against the memory of the man who had been so charming on the dance floor. 'Definitely glad you're driving me home and not him,' she added with a sigh. 'He's not a prize for anyone.'

Michael grinned but didn't reply, letting the conversation drift into quiet as the car descended further down the mountain. The air grew chillier as they neared Melbourne, the sun retreating behind the city skyline. When Michael finally pulled up to Bella's unit, she unfastened her seatbelt and turned to him with a tired but grateful smile. 'Thanks, Mick. It really was a great weekend.' He nodded, matching her smile. 'Back to reality now,' he said with a chuckle. Bella laughed softly, stepping out of the car. The memory of Danger Man's warmth lingered in her thoughts, but it didn't wipe away the memory of Leo's scowl and sharp words.

Chapter 3

Now Bella was back in her home she moved slowly from room to room, her overnight bag dangling limply from her hand. She dropped it by the bed, the zipper still closed. Exhaustion pulled at her, as she sank onto the couch, tension gripped her muscles, making her restless. She shifted, uncrossing her legs, then crossing them again. Clicking through channels, as if finding the right program might somehow settle her mind. But the hum of thoughts from the weekend refused to let her relax. Elsie and Steve's faces floated through her mind, faint and distant, like the sound of a far off aeroplane. She pictured them in the sky, miles away, growing further from her with every passing minute. The TV flickered, its images barely registering, just a blur of colour as memories tumbled in. Elsie's laugh. Steve's easy smile. Snapshots of the wedding. Bella's fingers flipped through the channels aimlessly, the remote clicking softly in the quiet room. The shrill whistle of the kettle pulled her into the kitchen. She poured steaming water into a mug, watching the swirl as she stirred. The silence in the kitchen felt louder somehow, wrapping itself around her. No more spontaneous visits from next door. No more late-night cups of tea with Elsie. A hollow ache spread through her chest.

The next morning brought relentless rain, a steady drumming on the roof that matched the rhythm of her heavy thoughts. Bella wandered through the house again, pausing by the window to watch the downpour sweep across her tiny front garden. Thin branches sagged under the weight of the water, bending low as gusts of wind pressed them closer to the ground. She exhaled slowly, her breath fogging the glass, but the heaviness in her chest didn't lift. It wasn't the rain. It was something deeper. A shift she couldn't yet name, looming over her like the storm clouds that darkened the sky. Change was coming. Whether it would arrive today, tomorrow, or next week, she didn't know, but its presence hovered, unspoken and unavoidable. Still at the window, she traced a finger along the cold glass, her thoughts turning to the past. She had felt this same weight once before. It was after her husband Harold passed away. His sudden death ten years ago from cancer had shattered her world, grief crashing in with flowers, casseroles, and murmured condolences. Back then, she had pushed through, finding purpose in her son, her job, the steady rhythm of daily life. Within weeks, she had returned to the office, forcing herself to keep moving. Keeping busy had made it easier to push the pain aside. But now, the silence pressed heavier, sharper. There were no distractions this time, no routine to anchor her. Only the stillness of the house and the memories that filled her mind. Not today, Bella thought, pulling her hand away from the window. She wasn't ready, not yet to face what lay ahead. She moved away from the window and drifted into the living room, hesitating as she passed the bookshelf. Her fingers skimmed along the spines of familiar titles—novels she had loved, travel guides filled with places she had once dreamed of visiting. A soft sigh left her lips. How long had it been since she had even considered the thought of adventure, of stepping beyond the boundaries of this small, predictable life? Too long.

Settling onto the couch, she tucked her feet beneath her and pulled a knitted throw over her lap. She stared at the silent TV, the reflections of rain running down the screen like ghostly figures. The house had never felt this empty before. It wasn't just about Elsie leaving. It was the weight of knowing there was no one left to break the quiet. Bella pressed a hand to her chest, as if trying to soothe the hollow space inside her. For years, she had moved through life with quiet resilience, picking up the pieces after Harold, building a life that was steady and safe. But now, that life suddenly felt like a waiting room, a place where time simply passed, rather than a world she was truly living in. A gust of wind rattled the windowpane, and Bella startled. She glanced toward the door, half-expecting someone to knock, someone to pull her out of this melancholy. But no one came. Of course, no one would. This was her reality now. But now, the silence pressed heavier, sharper. There were no distractions this time, no routine to anchor her. Only the stillness of the house and the memories that filled her mind. Not today. She inhaled deeply, her fingers tightening around the edge of the throw. Maybe she didn't have all the answers yet. Maybe she didn't know what came next. But she couldn't just sit here, letting the silence swallow her whole. With sudden resolve, she swung the blanket off her lap and stood. One step. Then another. Movement. A beginning, however small. She wasn't sure where she was going, but for now, just getting up, just deciding to move, was enough.

Chapter 4

Bella woke early and wandered through her unit, the stillness pressing against her like a weighted blanket. She dropped onto the couch, her gaze unfocused as her mind drifted to Elsie. Here mobile rang. Bella did not recognise the number she ignored it as if it was a sales call selling solar panels. She was soon back to her non stop self absorbed thinking. Elsie had been her life long friend from school days, their lives had been intertwined, friends closer than sisters. Together, they had sold the homes they'd once owned side by side, choosing units next to each other in the lifestyle village. There had never been secrets between them; Elsie knew Bella's heart better than anyone. And no one made Bella laugh the way Elsie could. Wild, fearless Elsie, who tackled life head-on and emerged from every challenge untouched. Mad as a hatter and fiercely loyal, Elsie had an uncanny way of walking into chaos and leaving without a speck of dust on her. Mountains were child's play for her; she scaled them without hesitation. Bella smiled faintly at the memory of Elsie's fiery resolve.

But now, the emptiness of the unit next door gnawed at her, the silence louder than any words. Each conversation Bella had in the village seemed to revolve around one word, one infuriating piece of advice: adjustment. Well-meaning residents repeated it like a mantra. 'It's part of life Bella; we all have to adjust.' Their reassurances, wrapped in smiles and nods, only weighed her down more. She muttered the word under her breath, frustration bubbling up. Adjustment. It settled in her chest like a stone, stirring up an urge to scream. She was sure she could murder the next person who mentioned that word. Rain streaked the window, tapping out an uneven rhythm that mirrored her restless thoughts. Her gaze wandered to the grey clouds outside, then her thoughts were of her old home. She could almost see her carefully tended roses, the neatly trimmed lawn. Memories of early mornings in the garden, the scent of fresh blooms, and the satisfaction of a job well done flooded her mind. It was all gone now, buried beneath a soulless block of grey flats. Bella shook her head, unwilling to dwell on the loss, but the ache remained, a persistent companion. She thought of Elsie again, off touring horse studs in Italy and France, sending photos and texts that briefly lifted Bella's spirits. A snapshot of rolling green hills, a cheeky caption about charming Italians, and Bella would smile, warmth blooming in her chest. But the joy always faded, leaving behind the same ache, the same grey-day feeling. Elsie had moved forward, as she always did, her spirit undiminished. And Bella? Bella was here, caught in the stillness, trying to figure out her next step. She stood and wandered into the bathroom, catching her reflection in the mirror. With a swipe of lipstick, she tried to shake off the melancholy. But the word *adjustment*, lingered in her mind. Had the people offering her advice ever faced the kind of loss she had? She doubted it. Their words felt hollow, a platitude for something they couldn't understand. 'Life changes, and we all have to adjust,' they'd say, as if change could be so neatly tied up in a word. Bella traced a finger along the edge of the mirror, her thoughts drifting to happier times. Why were these memories returning, did her mind purposely expose these emotions. Now, standing in the quiet of her living room, that same weight pressed on her. The world continued turning, but her life felt paused. She wasn't ready to face it yet. She sighed, rain continued to fall, the drops tracing uneven paths that matched her wandering thoughts. She'd tried to find ways to fill the void Elsie left behind, diving into village activities and making new friends. But nothing quite filled the old routine. Elsie's absence was a hollow she couldn't ignore.

Frustrated, she shook her head. This mood would pass, she told herself. It always did. Was it more difficult because she was older? Even as she tried to reassure herself, the weight of change loomed over her, heavy and unavoidable. Change had always been a part of life, she knew that. But knowing didn't make it easier. And today, all she knew was that she felt lonely. Outside, the storm clouds gathered, dark and unyielding. Bella watched the rain, her thoughts a quiet storm of their own. Somewhere out there, Elsie was conquering the world, her spirit as fierce and untamed as ever. Bella let out a soft sigh. She wasn't Elsie. But maybe, just maybe, she could find her own way forward when she was ready.

Chapter 5

When Bella went to check her mail at the community centre, a flyer stuck out of her mailbox. Curious, she pulled it free and unfolded it, her fingertips brushing over the crisp paper. The bold lettering announced a new indoor bowling club forming at the community hall. The details explained that George, one of the residents, had organised the equipment for carpet bowls and was inviting anyone interested to join. As Bella read, the idea piqued her thoughts. Maybe I'll try it. She came across George on her way back, and asked him about the indoor Bowles.

'How many takers do you think you will get?

'Ten to twelve, I'd guess,' he replied, his tone light yet matter-of-fact. '

'Hope so.' Bella stated. 'It's nice of you to arrange this, George.' 'Selfish, really.' George added with a half-smile, 'I've played for years, mostly outdoors. Great fun. Indoors should be just as good.' 'I am putting my name down to have a try.' Bella said.

'That's good Bella, I hope you like it. I have stored all

the equipment up in the community room, so I will be setting it up next week.'

'Good to have something new to try, thanks George.' Normally, she would've popped over to Elsie's with the flyer in hand, knowing her best friend would be just as curious. They'd settle on Elsie's couch or out on the porch, tea or wine between them, laughing over the idea of their knees giving out during a round of bowls. A small smile tugged at Bella's lips as she pictured the scene. Elsie's teasing voice echoing in her ears, 'Well, can you even bend that far anymore?' The clink of their glasses and the warmth of Elsie's laughter filled her imagination. But when Bella looked toward the empty porch next door, her smile faded. The stillness reminded her of what was gone. No Elsie to laugh with, no easy afternoons shared over quiet confidences. For a moment, her heart ached, wondering how she would ever fill the void left by Elsie's absence.

The cheerful design of the flyer now felt like a gauntlet thrown at her feet, daring her to step into a new world on her own. The prospect of indoor bowling danced in the back of her mind like a welcome distraction, yet a shadow of doubt loomed. Was she ready to embrace this change, to make decisions without Elsie's input? The word adjustment drifted through her thoughts, bitter and unwelcome. With a deep, steadying breath, Bella realised this wasn't just another community activity. It was the first decision she'd have to make entirely on her own, a small but significant step into the unknown. She pressed the flyer against her chest, feeling the cool paper as if it were a promise of both new beginnings and the inevitable heartache of moving forward. When Bella went to drop off her filled in flyer for indoor bowls, she spotted Connie from the notoriously strict golfers' club.

The group had a reputation that preceded it. Members as loyal to their sport as knights to a code. They took their club seriously, too seriously, in Bella's opinion, but it was the largest group in the village, and its influence was hard to ignore. 'What do you think of the new indoor bowls?' Bella asked, keeping her tone casual.

'Not much,' Connie replied with a shrug. 'Can't compare it to the thrill of golf, of course.'

'Probably like most sports, it depends on good hand-eye coordination,' Bella mused, though her thoughts immediately wandered to Elsie. She could almost hear her friend's voice chiming in: Girly game. Not like tennis, where you can slam the ball hard, hit your annoying o

'I'm giving it a try, see what it's like,' she said, more to herself than to Connie.

'Brave you,' Connie said with a condescending chuckle. 'Apparently George has been in bowling clubs half his life,' Bella added. 'He's offered to teach anyone new.'

'That's nice of him,' Connie said, her eyes twinkling with feint praise. Then it came. 'Heard from Elsie?' Connie asked casually. Bella immediately tensed. There it was, the dreaded name, slipping into conversation like it was nothing. Bella braced herself, irritation flaring like a match struck in a dry room. Elsie, Elsie, Elsie. Could the universe let her go one day without a reminder?

'She's in France, looking at racehorses,' Bella replied. Connie continued, sighing dreamily.

'Nice European honeymoon, lucky girl. Photos from the wedding were so natural. Such a beautiful place to get married. All those horses and paddocks. Would you do it again, Bella?'

Bella shrugged her shoulders. 'I'll let you know if someone ever asks me.'

'Same here,' Connie laughed. 'Everyone around here's either taken or about to book a room in heaven. Doesn't leave us girls with much choice, does it?' Connie leaned in, her expression softening. 'Elsie really is the luckiest girl in the world to find someone to marry.'

Bella clenched her teeth. There it was again. And then came the inevitable: 'Hope you won't take this the wrong way Bella, but adjusting to Elsie moving away... it's bound to be hard.' Adjusting. Bella's jaw tightened as Connie prattled on, her syrupy advice pouring over her

Chapter 6

As Connie and Bella walked back to their homes, Bella 's gaze wandered to the manicured hedges and uniform cream shutters of the village units. She focused on counting her breaths, trying to smother the rising irritation.

'The golf girls and I were talking the other night,' Connie continued, her tone now conspiratorial, 'and we've got just the idea for you.'

'Mmm,' Bella murmured, wary.

'We thought you might like to join us at the club. A part membership to start, just until you're through this lonely stage.' Lonely stage? Bella's fingers curled into fists.

'You don't have to decide now,' Connie added brightly. 'Just be ready on Wednesday at nine we'll pick you up for training. Bernadette's offered to lend you some of her golfing outfits. Gorgeous pieces, and she's about your size. You'll look fabulous!' Bella's mouth opened, but all that came out was a muffled, 'Oh.' Connie beamed, oblivious.

'We're betting you'll fall in love with golf. It's a game you can't help but want to play every day!' Bella barely resisted the urge to snap. Instead, she muttered, 'Uh-huh,' while her mind screamed. Connie continued, her imagination clearly racing ahead to Bella's transformation into a devoted golfer.

'Murder,' Bella muttered through gritted teeth, the word slipping out before she could stop it.

Connie frowned, puzzled. 'Bella, are you okay? What's murder got to do with golf?'

'When I first retired I had lesson's in golf, and at the first tournament I came fourth. The coach said I was a natural.' Connie's face took on an astounded expression. 'That's wonderful our team needs a heavy hitter.'

Bella straightened quickly, recovering. 'It's just... my back. My surgeon said golf could make it worse, might even require surgery.' 'Oh, which vertebra?' Connie asked, launching into a long-winded analysis of sports injuries, offering advice Bella hadn't asked for.

'No,' Bella interrupted sharply. 'I can't play golf.' Her voice rose slightly, surprising even herself. Connie blinked, taken aback. 'That's hardly fair.'

'Who to? Bella stood her ground.

'But with your natural talent …

'No golf,' Bella whispered, her voice now dangerously calm. By the time Bella reached her front door, she'd decided no more chats with her neighbours, especially not the golfing crowd. On Wednesday morning, she stayed in bed, ignoring the persistent knocking from the golf ladies outside.

Chapter 7

Bella realised she needed other friends at the lifestyle village. Maybe it was time to join more activities to fill her days. Spotting a group through the window heading toward the community centre, she opened her door. 'Jan, what's on today?' Bella called out. 'Hello, Bella! How was the wedding?' Jan replied, her bright smile as warm as the morning sun.

'Great!' Bella said, a genuine smile surfacing.

'We're having a meeting about going on holiday. Want to come and see if it interests you?'

Bella nodded and joined the group as they strolled to the community meeting room. Her curiosity stirred, and for the first time in weeks, she felt a flicker of excitement. Inside, Jan stepped to the front, addressing a lively group of residents.

'We've decided to plan a group trip!' she announced, her voice brimming with enthusiasm. 'Some singles, some couples, it should be a blast. What do you think, Bella?'

'Count me in,' Bella said, her spirits lifting at the

thought of a getaway. Jan grabbed a marker and began jotting ideas on a whiteboard. 'Alright, let's brainstorm. Where to?'

'Great Barrier Reef!' someone called out.

'Tasmania!' chimed another voice.

'Hamilton Island, or maybe New Zealand!'

Alf cleared his throat dramatically. 'I've got relatives in Perth...' One of the golf ladies quipped, 'What are you suggesting, Alf? That we all bunk in with your family?' The room erupted in laughter, and Alf shrugged, grinning.

'Alright, alright, scratch that one.' Jan waved her marker in mock warning. 'Focus, everyone. How long do we want?' 'Eight to ten days sounds perfect,' Connie suggested. After a quick vote, the group settled on five nights and six days, long enough to feel like a real holiday without exhausting anyone. The destination ideas narrowed to four options: The Ghan to Darwin, the Indian Pacific across Australia, a guided tour abroad, or a cruise. Each suggestion sparked lively chatter. In the end, the cruise won out. The group decided on The Splendor of the Sea, departing from Sydney just weeks away, with a route through tropical islands.

The time leading up to the trip buzzed with excitement. Passports were unearthed from dusty drawers, and casual morning teas transformed into packing discussions. 'What shoes work best for morning walks on deck?' someone wondered aloud. Two ladies proudly displayed their brand-new suitcases, one a blinding iridescent green, the

'At least you won't lose them at the baggage carousel,' Bella said, chuckling. Across the room, a quiet husband leaned toward his wife and whispered, 'Pack your own case, though. Last thing we need is a customs stop.' His wife rolled her eyes. 'As if you even know where the bags are kept.'

'I know enough to bring them in from the garage,' he retorted, barely hiding his grin.

'Good. So we're not worried about smuggling contraband then?' someone joked, earning laughter from the group. Jan leaned forward, her enthusiasm infectious. 'And think of all the new foods we can try!' Let's be adventurous and all try something different. Jan put forward. There was total agreement in the group. 'It's no use going and not experiencing the international cuisine.' said one gent.' The traveler's' eyes lit up, imagining balmy seas and exotic dishes.

Stories flowed about past trips, and those who hadn't been to Noumea eagerly speculated about their first impressions. A local travel agent was enlisted to handle logistics, arranging flights to Sydney and booking the cruise. With every passing day, the excitement grew. When the departure date finally arrived, Bella found herself packing with a grin. She placed the last item in her suitcase, snapped it shut, and set it by the door. The buzz of anticipation filled her mind. The fun's already begun, she thought, ready to step into this new adventure with her friends.

Chapter 8

The bus pulled up in front of the community hall, and the driver began loading luggage as the traveler's clustered together, their voices overlapping with excitement. The airport trip flew by, and before long, they were boarding the hour-long flight to Sydney. Anticipation bubbled as a private bus whisked them from Sydney Airport to the Overseas Passenger Terminal at Circular Quay. Tunnels zipped past, then sunlight glinted off city buildings, adding to the buzz as they dragged their cases through the bustling terminal.

And then they saw it, The Splendor of the Sea, towering like a gleaming white colossus against the midday sun. Bella's eyes widened, marvelling at its sheer size as the group made their way toward the boarding area.

A photographer intercepted them, corralling each person in front of a pull up photo backdrop featuring palm trees. 'Smile,' he said, his voice tinged with the weariness of a thousand repetitions that day.

In the check-in line, customs officials in navy suits

called, 'Papers, please.' Robert and Beryl began a hushed argument over the location of their passports.

'Where'd you put them?' Beryl asked, arms crossed, her tone sharpened to a fine edge.

Robert rummaged through his pockets, growing more flustered by the second. 'They might be in your handbag,' he muttered weakly.

Beryl sighed, clearly unimpressed, and stepped forward in line. Moments later, Robert dropped to his knees, his suitcase sprawled open on the terminal floor.

'Found them,' he called out, triumphantly pulling the passports from a netted lining in the bag's lid.

Beryl rolled her eyes. 'Hurry up, Robert, you're holding up the queue.'

The passengers shuffled single file down a narrow walk way. The boarding process dragged, and Bella felt a flicker of exhaustion by the time she finally reached the lifts. Floor numbers, cabin numbers, and directions blurred together as announcements blared in the background.

After what felt like a mini-marathon, Bella located her single cabin. Meanwhile, the golf ladies paired off in shared rooms. By then, a celebratory drink was non-negotiable.

The group reconvened in the lounge, raising glasses to toast their adventure. Bella glanced out the window, captivated by the orange sun casting a golden glow over Sydney's skyline. Out on deck, other passengers sipped cocktails, marvelling at the swirling sunset hues painting the sky like an artist's masterpiece.

Next on the agenda was exploring the ship. Some gravitated toward the casino, while others wandered through the onboard shops. Bella's eye caught a flyer advertising high tea, and as a devoted cake enthusiast, she quickly booked a

Wednesday slot. Six others eagerly joined, already excited to sample the treats.

Dinner presented its own set of challenges, starting with the choice between early and late seating. Bella noticed a long queue of silver-haired guests pushing walkers, eagerly awaiting the early option.

'Not tonight,' someone murmured, and the group unanimously agreed on the later seating.

Finally seated at a round table, they pored over the dinner menu, an array of exotic choices staring back at them: squid, frogs' legs, escargot, and mussels prepared in various ways. It was one thing to chat about trying exotic food in the safety of your own home—but choosing to put it into your mouth was another matter entirely.

Reactions were immediate—and hilariously unfiltered.

'Not touching those slimy little devils,' Syd grumbled, squinting over his menu.

'They're very French,' said Jan, wrinkling her nose, 'but no thanks.' 'What about mussels?' someone ventured.

'They look... unwashed,' came the quiet reply. They all held the menu's and kept reading, the quietness was broken by Beryl suddenly declaring in a loud voice.

'Roast lamb and veggies for me,' A chorus of 'good choice,' quickly followed, solidifying the group's safe dinner choice for their first night at sea.

As the ship sailed into open waters, Bella felt herself relaxing into the adventure. The chaos of packing, boarding, and navigating the unfamiliar had given way to camaraderie and laughter a happy start to the journey ahead.

Chapter 9

The morning sun gleamed off the ship's polished railings as passengers clustered around the main gallery wall, laughing at their arrival photos. The air buzzed with playful complaints, 'I look terrible!' followed by friendly jabs and chuckles. 'That's a nice one of you,' someone pointed out. Bella passed by as Connie stepped back from the display.

'Hi, Bella. There's a beautiful photo of you boarding the ship. Just over there.'

'No thanks, Connie. I don't need any photos of me,' Bella said, shaking her head. Unfazed, Connie smiled. 'We're all going to a gemstone workshop at eleven on the second floor. Want to join us?'

Bella hesitated, then lifted the book in her hand. 'I was going somewhere quiet to read, but gems sound interesting.'

The workshop room buzzed with excitement, every chair filled. At the front, a jeweller held up a dazzling blue stone. 'This is a Tanzanite,' he announced, his voice rich with enthusiasm. He gestured to a map of Africa, tapping a tiny red dot. 'Found only in this small region, nowhere else on Earth. They rival diamonds in rarity.' As trays of deep blue rings circulated, murmurs of admiration spread through the room.

'I'm getting one,' Jan declared, her eyes gleaming. Bella smiled but shook her head.

'Not much into jewellery. I don't need any rings.' After the workshop, Bella drifted to the outer deck, inhaling the briny air. The sea stretched in an unbroken expanse of grey blue, its surface shifting with slow, rhythmic swells. She stared at the horizon, feeling the emptiness press in. No birds. No boats. Just endless water. A familiar pang of loneliness settled in her chest. She opened her book, forcing herself to focus. But the words blurred.

She read the same sentence three times before snapping it shut. Why do I feel so alone in the middle of an adventure? she wondered. The silence around her deepened, mirroring the quiet ache inside.

The next day, anticipation rippled through the ship as they anchored near a tropical island. Passengers eagerly boarded tenders, the scent of salt and flowers thick in the warm breeze. Islanders greeted them with easy smiles. The market bustled with stalls of vibrant crafts, while locals sliced open fresh coconuts, handing them to eager travellers.

Bella let the island's charm wash over her. The sun warmed her skin; the crystal-clear waves lapped at her feet. For the first time in days, her thoughts quieted. But as the tenders ferried them back to the ship, a wistful longing crept in.

That evening, over dinner, the cruise staff announced a raffle winner. 'Beryl, you'll be dining at the captain's table tonight!' The dining hall erupted in applause.

Beryl beamed. 'This is the best moment of my trip!'

'What an honour,' Jan added.

Bella smiled faintly. 'I'm heading to a movie on the deck.' By the time she arrived, the pool deck was packed, most lounge chairs claimed. She found one midway along and stretched out, eager to lose herself in the film. The sky had deepened to velvet, the ocean a silent abyss beyond the railing.

Just as she settled in, Bob and Terry from her lifestyle village spotted her and plopped down in front of her.

'What's the movie about, Bella?' Bob asked.

'Yeah, tell us,' Terry added. 'Want a drink?'

'No, thanks,' Bella said, firm but polite. Bob shifted closer, forcing nearby guests to adjust their seats. 'Nice to have you to myself,' he said, patting her leg.

Bella stiffened, pulling away. 'What does that mean, Bob?'

'I just mean you're always surrounded by people. I'd like to ask you to dinner sometime.'

'No, thank you.'

'Well, just as friends, then?'

'No, Bob. I'm not interested.'

'Okay, maybe after the movie? A few of us are having drinks in my cabin.'

'Early night for me. I need my beauty sleep.'

Bob leaned in. 'Has anyone told you how beautiful you are?' Bella kept her eyes on the screen.

'Not today.'

'Well, in my opinion, you're the best-looking lady in our village.' His hand inched toward her leg again. 'I heard from the girls that it'll be hard for you with Elsie gone. You'll need to adjust.'

Bella's patience snapped. She turned sharply. 'Which

girls, Bob?' He hesitated, feigning interest in the movie. 'Which girls?' she demanded.

'Uh, just the golf club ladies,' he muttered. Bella shot to her feet, her voice slicing through the night. 'Let me make this clear: I don't want to date you or anyone. I hate golf. I'm on this cruise to relax, not to have my life analysed. Now, Bob… PISS OFF!'

Gasps rippled through the deck. Bella strode away, her pulse hammering. As she reached her cabin, she leaned against the door, exhaling slowly. Enough. Enough of the gossip, the meddling, the expectations. She'd cut ties if necessary. Tomorrow was a new day, a fresh start.

Chapter 10

Bella decided the high tea tomorrow would be the moment she confronted the golf ladies. She envisioned her words sharp and direct, delivered just after they had eaten their last petit four.

The table was impeccably set with polished silver and gleaming white plates. At the centre stood silver-tiered cake stands adorned with an array of bite-sized cakes. Each was a miniature work of art, with vibrant colours and intricate decorations that made choosing the first one almost impossible. As the waiter poured tea and served the cakes, Bella selected a passionfruit-topped square. With the first bite, a surprising hint of ginger burst onto her taste buds. Around her, the other women savoured their selections, describing the delicate flavours and exquisite presentation.

'Delightful, and so beautifully decorated,' Pam said, marvelling at the chef's skill. The group chatted about the patience it must take to create such tiny masterpieces. The chef who prepared the spread came to the table answering questions about the cakes. Bella didn't waste any time asking what ingredients went into the passionfruit-topped square. 'I love to bake cakes, and I have never tasted anything like it before.' The chef was very helpful and gave Bella the ingredient list. As the ladies were finishing their last petit four, Bella drew in a long breath. Individually each of the ladies were pleasant, nice people. However together they formed a formidable enemy, and Bella knew she must express how she was feeling.

Bella tapped her spoon on her glass. The gentle clink drew their attention, and the table quieted. 'I want to share something with you all,' Bella began, her voice calm but firm. Her face remained unreadable.

Pam frowned, leaning forward. 'Whatever is wrong?' Bella glanced around the table, her gaze lingering on each woman before settling on Connie. Her voice grew stronger and louder, ensuring she was heard.

'Ladies, let me make something clear. I do not want to date.' She paused, watching their reactions. 'I hate golf.' Another pause. No one moved a muscle. The room was still.

Bella continued, 'I don't want to wear another woman's clothes, and I certainly don't want to be told I'll be picked up at nine a.m. for golf practice without being asked.' She pointed at Connie. 'All of this was orchestrated by you. Yes, *you*, Connie. You have taken it upon yourself to organise my life. If I hear the word 'adjustment' one more time, I swear I'll smack the speaker in the face.' The women were stunned, and a heavy silence hung over the table.

'I came on this cruise to relax, not to be analyzed by a group of gossipy, self-appointed life planners. At home, I tolerated it, even though it was in poor taste. But here, on a holiday? You've crossed the line.'

Connie looked up, her eyes wide, and then broke into

tears. Her hands flew to her face, muffling her sobs. Someone handed her a napkin, which she clutched as she cried harder.

Through her tears, Connie stammered, 'Bella, I'm so, so sorry. I never thought I was hurting you.'

'Hurting me? More like taking over my life,' Bella shot back. 'I didn't mean to.'

'Shush Connie allow me to speak. Yes, you did, you project managed the whole thing. How would you feel if I did this to you?' Bella's voice rose. 'Do you think you're above reproach, Connie? Above gossip? You're like a farmer spreading manure on a crop except your crop is people's lives, and you spread gossip instead of seeds.'

Connie sobbed harder. 'I didn't think I told anyone except the golf girls.'

'Oh, so that's what you're worried about? Who you told, not who you hurt?' Bella's tone grew sharper. 'Do you honestly think gossip stays contained? That the golf girls keep their secrets locked away? Even here, in the middle of the ocean, your meddling inspired Bob and Terry to proposition me on deck. They thought I needed a boyfriend to help me 'adjust.' Who told them that? One of you?' Bella raised her finger and pointed at each of the group. The women sat frozen, staring at Connie or the table, too stunned to speak.

Bella's voice softened slightly but retained its edge. 'This goes for all of you. Connie isn't the only one guilty here. You all connived, showing just how 'organised' you can be at someone else's expense. Maybe next time, think twice before you interfere in someone's life without their consent.'

Bella slowly pushed her chair back and stood. She cast a deliberate, lingering look at each woman before turning and walking away without another word. In her cabin,

Bella collapsed onto the bed, the day's emotions crashing over her. She burst into tears the kind of deep, soul, cleansing cry she hadn't allowed herself in ages. Loneliness washed over her, mingling with the frustration of missing her old life. She hadn't asked for advice. She didn't want it.

This was her journey, her burden to carry, and she knew it. Today she had reclaimed some of her personal power. The golf ladies knew exactly where they stood with her now. Bella's speech had been necessary, not just to set boundaries, but to remind herself of her own strength. And for the first time in a long while, she felt the faintest glimmer of relief.

Chapter 11

Bella began a new regime, swimming in the morning to keep fit. Joining the indoor bowls and learning a new sport was good for her mind. The others that joined were not trying to win Wimbledon, or a cup. They were just having some fun. With an activity planned for each day, she was starting to feel alive again. Mingling with a different group of friends at the lifestyle village brought a new sense of happiness. Meanwhile, cards and text messages from Elsie and Steve remained a source of joy.

One afternoon, Bella's phone rang, displaying an unfamiliar number. Annoyed by frequent sales calls, she ignored it. When the sam

'Hello,' she said.

'Is that Bella?'

'Yes, that's me.'

The voice was husky and warm, but unfamiliar. 'Hi, Bella, it's Leo here.'

'Oh, hello, Leo. Calling to tell me not to give the horses an apple?' she replied, her tone edged with dry humour.

There was a pause, followed by the sound of him drawing a breath.

'I'm in Melbourne today and was wondering if you'd like to have a coffee with me. I want to apologise for how rude I was the last time we met.'

'Oh,' said Bella. 'I don't know which Leo I'd be meeting, the charming wedding man or the grumpy apple man.'

'Please, let's have a coffee and catch up,' he said, his tone softening. 'Sure,' Bella replied, though her voice remained flat.

'Where do you live, Bella?' She considered giving a flippant answer like 'the zoo' or 'Timbuktu' but decided to be civil. After all, Leo was trying to be pleasant. She gave him her address, and he mentioned he was nearby and could be there in half an hour. 'Okay,' Bella said before ending the call.

Watching through the window, Bella saw his car pull up in front of her unit. As he stepped out, she noted his tall, muscular physique. He wore a crisp white collarless shirt and grey trousers. When she opened the door, she was momentarily struck by how handsome he was. His clean-shaven face bore fine features, and his broad smile radiated warmth.

'Come in, Leo,' Bella said. 'How do you take your coffee?'

'Black with sugar,' he replied. Bella had already set out a vanilla sponge cake, and they sat at the dining table. She sliced it and offered him a plate. She worked hard to keep the mood light as they chatted about horses and the wedding.

'Bill told me I was rough on you,' Leo said eventually, his expression earnest. 'I want to say I'm sorry, Bella. I had no excuse for being so sarcastic. It was an outside matter that threw me off that day.'

'Yes.' Bella studied him, noticing how his hair curled in a way that gave him a relaxed, almost boyish charm. She shook her head inwardly, handsome but caustic.

'What brings you down the mountain?' she asked.

'I had family matters to attend to,' Leo explained. 'My eldest daughter graduated today as a nurse, so we all went to the ceremony.'

'I didn't think you were married,' Bella said, curiosity flickering in her tone.

'I'm definitely not,' Leo replied. 'But my ex and I go to all family events involving the kids to present a united front. We try to do what's best for them, even though they're adults now.'

'That's nice,' Bella said. Leo raised an eyebrow and tilted his head. 'Sometimes,' he replied with a faint smirk.

'Do you have kids, Bella?'

'So, I guess you don't see him often.'

'Not often, unfortunately,' Bella said. 'But we talk regularly, and I get plenty of photos of my granddaughter.'

'Life can end up in a mess sometimes, can't it?' Leo remarked.

'Yes, we never know what's around the corner,' Bella agreed. 'Bella,' Leo began, 'we're having a p

'Not really. I don't drive anymore,' Bella said, noting the flash of disappointment that crossed his face.

'There are a few people coming up from Melbourne,' Leo said quickly. 'They'd be happy to give you a lift. Most of them are staying overnight. You don't have to decide now. I'll call you later in the week to check.'

'Well, you have my number. I'll think about it,' Bella replied.

Leo left, feeling as though he'd barely scratched the surface of Bella's reserve. As he drove back to the stud farm, his mind wandered to her. Her dark curls framed her face in a way that captivated him. He shook his head, regretting the way he'd treated her over the horses. There was no excuse, only the lingering frustration of a tense phone call with his ex about the graduation arrangements. Taking it out on Bella had been unforgivable.

Meanwhile, Bella mulled over the invitation. After the cruise debacle, the prospect of meeting and socialising with new people felt exciting. She thought of Leo's warm voice and striking appearance. The idea of attending the party seemed even more tempting. Still, she reminded herself of his brusque demeanour during their meeting with Danger Man and hoped it had been an isolated incident. Besides she was feeling very attracted to him.

Chapter 12

On Thursday, Bella glanced at her ringing phone, Leo's name flashed on the screen. She hesitated, a familiar mix of curiosity and uncertainty stirring within her, then she answered.

'Hi, Bella, how are you?' he greeted her.

'I'm good,' Bella replied, her mixed emotions bubbling to the surface. She was still unsure of Leo.

'We've had a breakthrough with Velvet Glow,' he said, a touch of pride in his voice. 'She's out in the paddock now with her first group of racehorses.'

'Oh, that's promising,' Bella said, her interest piqued.

'The trainer's been working with her one-on-one, and she's really responding. When the others take off, she's right there with them now. She stays with the herd.' His enthusiasm resonated through the line.

Bella stifled the urge to bring up the apple incident and decided against it. 'How's Danger Man doing?'

'Still shining, as magnificent as ever.' Leo's voice softened, as if picturing the horse in his mind.

'He's a wonder, Bella.' After a pause, he added, 'Have you thought any more about coming to our party?'

'Celebrating something special?' she asked, leaning back in her chair.

'Actually, it's my birthday.' Leo's voice dropped a little, almost shy. Bella smiled to herself.

'Well, I'd better make an appearance then.' 'You'll have a good time; we're bringing in the same band we had at Steve and Elsie's wedding. You did love their music.'

Her own excitement began to build. 'That band? Well, they are a great band, I do love dancing.'

'I remember.' Leo said with a laugh in his voice. Bella realised she was looking forward to seeing the horses again, and maybe even finding the happy dancing Leo. Leo happily took her response as a yes. 'How about I pick you up around 1:30 on Friday?'

'Sounds good,' Bella agreed, a touch of warmth creeping into her voice.

Chapter 13

Bella ordered a taxi to the shopping centre, determined to find a gift for Leo. Picking out a card was easy, but the gift itself proved tricky. Her mind kept circling back to horses, but surely he had everything he could ever need related to them. She wandered through the aisles of gift shops, and major chain stores menswear departments, hoping for inspiration to strike. Finally, something caught her eye, and she decided it was perfect. She grabbed a trolley, loaded her purchase, and made her way to the taxi rank.

When the driver placed her bags into the boot, he raised an eyebrow. 'This box is a bit heavy luv,' he remarked. Bella just smiled, feeling satisfied with her choice. She spent the rest of the day wrapping the gift and packing for the weekend. She decided to make her Dreamy Chocolate sponge cake it was by far her most popular. By Friday, she was all ready. When Leo's c

'Hello, Bella. I'm so glad you decided to come.' She let a playful smile slip. 'I'm only going to see Velvet Glow. I missed her last time.'

Leo laughed, his expression warm. 'She's in the south paddock waiting for you. I told her you'd be visiting.'

The drive out to the Macedon Ranges flew by as they chatted. Bella couldn't help feeling at ease, enjoying their conversation. 'Expecting a lot of people at your party?' she asked. 'About fifty. We're having a spit roast, and Cook's handling everything. He's the best around.'

'Oh, good I made my Dreamy Chocolate sponge. It's in the container in the boot.'

Leo's eyebrows lifted, impressed. 'Do you like cooking, Bella? Sponges are my forte.' 'Well, I claim the first slice!' he laughed.

When they arrived at the stud, the place buzzed with energy. Horses moved about, riders galloped along the track, and workers bustled everywhere. As they unpacked, Leo eyed the brightly coloured gift, chuckling.

'This one's heavy. Hope it's not the sponge.'

'Nope, it's safe in the container,' Bella replied, pleased he'd noticed the present. After settling into her room, Bella wandered back out to find Leo waiting in the kitchen area. She watched him, taking in his familiar ease in his surroundings.

'Leo, where do you live, by the way?' He pointed down a valley past the training track. 'Can't see my house from here, but I'll show you.' They hopped into his vehicle and drove through the estate, passing workers and other staff who waved as they went. Bella took in the friendly vibe

'Bill's my dad. His brother Fred is Steve's dad, so we're all cousins. We share equal stakes in the stud, which keeps things smooth. It was our grandfathers' idea to make it a shared venture.'

Bella looked around, trying to imagine it. 'Seems rare these days.' He shrugged with a grin. 'It works. Everything's open. Equal wages, equal shares. There've been lean years when we worked off-property just to keep things going. But we're still here.'

They wound down a hill as Leo pointed out more of their land. 'Down there is my house, though it's emptier now. My dad moved back after my divorce. The girls' rooms are still there for when they visit.' As they approached, Bella caught sight of the house, a sprawling Federation home, brick structure surrounded by a garden that looked fit for a postcard. Leo drove down the main driveway, stopping near the front door. The wide verandah was dotted with potted plants, and table's and chairs. Inside, the huge kitchen caught her attention first. Bella admired the room's warmth and openness, especially the central island and the very large oven.

'It's a beautiful home,' she shared with Leo.

'Let me show you around.' Leo led her through the hall, explaining that one end housed his dad's quarters and the girls' rooms. The tour took them to sliding glass doors that opened out to a patio, complete with a pool, spa, and changing room.

Bella chuckled. 'Hope that pool is not for the horses.'

'Nope, that's for us,' he said, grinning. 'The spa's perfect on winter nights. Laying back star gazing, we get great sights of comets. There is no smog up here, so the stars we see from up here are so clear.'

As they talked, Leo's phone rang. 'Hello, Evelyn. What? No, they'll need to sort it themselves.' His tone grew short. 'Definitely not.' Bella wandered around the patio, admiring the carefully tended garden. Leo came out, his face flushed.

'That was my ex,' he said, the words clipped. Bella let the silence settle, walking past the gar

'That was the plan,' he replied, his voice softening. A

short silence passed, then he turned to her with a smile. 'Come with me, Bella. I have a surprise for you.' Intrigued, she followed him across the lawn and through a small grove of white gum trees. They reached a fenced paddock, and Bella gasped, her heart skipping as she recognised the glossy chestnut coat of Velvet Glow.

'Oh, Velvet Glow!' She beamed, moving to the gate Leo pointed to. Leo chuckled, clearly pleased by her reaction.

'She's here today just for you.' As Bella approached the horse, she felt a swell of joy. 'Do you remember me, Velvet Glow?' she cooed, reaching out to scratch behind the mare's ear. 'I was at your first race! You came in fourth.' Leo joined her, watching as Velvet Glow leaned into Bella's hand.

'You do love horses,' he murmured, smiling as the mare nuzzled her. Bella rubbed Velvet Glow's soft nose, feeling warmth bloom in her chest. 'I remember the jockey saying she was smart and steady on the track. Has she raced since then?'

'No, we've focused on strength training and early rides with other horses to get her used to the track.' Bella nodded, patting Velvet Glow's flank, feeling the horse's sleek muscles under her hand. 'She's a beauty. Thanks for letting me spend time with her.' Leo's eyes softened.

'I'm so glad you are here, Bella.

For a moment they stood in comfortable silence, Bella enjoying Velvet Glow's company and the quiet warmth of Leo nearby.

Chapter 14

They drove slowly up to the main house. The beauty of the stud farm was evident at every glance. Established over a century ago, each generation had added to its charm, creating a place that exuded both history and elegance.

'Thank you for bringing the chocolate sponge cake, Bella. Would you mind if I used it as the birthday cake for Leo?' Cook asked as they stepped into the bustling kitchen.

'Not at all,' Bella replied with a smile.

'Great, then I get the first slice,' Leo added from behind them, making them both chuckle.

'It's huge,' Cook noted, eyeing the cake approvingly.

'I always make extra large ones these days, everyone wants seconds.'

Outside, guests were arriving in steady streams. Some wandered down to Leo's house, while others stayed near the main house. The parking area filled quickly, and the band set up beneath the towering gum trees, tuning their instruments in the warm evening air.

Bella mingled effortlessly, chatting with guests about

their travels, horses, and the equestrian world. She fit in easily, surprising even herself. Leo soon found her amidst the crowd, his gaze softening when he spotted her.

'Bella how are you doing?' he asked, with a huge smile.

'We've adopted her,' one of his friends interjected with a grin.

'It's unusual for a city girl to be so interested in horses,' another noted.

A broad smile crossed Leo's face. 'Bella has Danger Man on speed dial.' Laughter rippled through the group. Leo slid his arm around Bella, and she felt his warmth. She glanced up at him, drawn in once again by his ruggedly handsome features.

'Come with me Bella. Bill says I've been hiding you away. He's outside.'

'Bill, hello!' Bella greeted warmly, giving him a quick hug.

'How have you been?'

'Better now that I've seen you,' he teased, making her laugh. Leo handed her a drink, watching the easy interaction between them. Leo stood back for a moment, quietly observing Bella. The way she moved, how naturally she engaged with others, he was captivated.

He hadn't felt this way in years. His past, however, loomed close behind.

A voice interrupted the peace.

'Leo, happy birthday.'

His face paled instantly. 'What the...' he muttered under his breath.

Three women walked into the party. Two young, beautiful women threw their arms around Leo's neck. 'Happy birthday, Dad!' His expression transformed as he spun them around, laughing. 'My girls!' The warmth of the moment dissipated when the third woman stepped forward.

'Happy birthday, Leo,' Evelyn purred.

She moved in, attempting to plant a kiss on his cheek, but he stepped back, his eyes darkening with anger.

'What the hell are you doing here, Evelyn?'

'Nice for the family to be together on your birthday,' she said smoothly, flicking a glance around. She was dressed to kill. Red, figure-hugging dress, plunging neckline, gold jewellery at every available space.

Leo stiffened. Bill, standing nearby, leaned toward Bella and whispered, 'Go check if Cook needs help. This is going to get messy, and you won't want to be in the crossfire.' Bella nodded and slipped into the kitchen

'Wow!' Cook exclaimed as she entered. 'Has the furniture started flying yet?'

Bella laughed. 'Not yet, but Bill thought it was a good idea for me to disappear.'

'Smart man,' Cook said. 'Evelyn loves an audience.'

Right on cue, a loud noise echoed from outside, followed by Evelyn's screeching voice. An argument had begun.

Leo's daughters, Chloe and Sarah, strolled in, unfazed.

'Hungry as usual?' Cook asked knowingly.

'Always,' Chloe grinned, opening the fridge. 'What's good?' 'Bolognese and pasta, second shelf,' Cook answered. 'Might keep you full till dinner.' The sisters playfully elbowed each other, laughing as they grabbed plates.

'Girls, this is Bella,' Cook introduced.

'Hi, Bella,' they chimed in unison.

Chloe smirked. 'We're the kids with the mother from hell out there.'

'Now, now,' Bill chided as he entered.

'Grandpa, you know what happens if Mum doesn't get her way.' 'We all do,' Cook chuckled.

Sarah shrugged. 'She wasn't invited. She couldn't stand being left out. Who's staying at our place?' Chloe asked.

'Not sure yet,' Bill admitted. 'Your mum needs to leave, though. Your aunty Janet's only ten minutes away.'

'Nice try, Grandpa. She won't go quietly.'

Outside, Evelyn's voice cut through the night air. 'Fine, I'll go, since I'm not welcome here.'

Bill pulled out his phone.

'Janet, we've got trouble.'

'Evelyn?'

'Yep. She's in a mood.'

'I'll expect her.'

'Thanks, Janet.'

Leo stormed into the kitchen, firmly holding onto Evelyn's wrist, guiding her to the door. 'Evelyn, get into your car and leave.'

'You can't make me Leo. My girls are here.'

'You weren't invited. You have no reason to be here.'

'Who's staying at your house?'

'None of your business.'

Bill followed them outside. 'Janet is expecting you. It's a short drive, and you haven't been drinking. Best you go.'

Evelyn glared at them as she walked to her car. Leo opened the car door, and she reluctantly got in. With a rev of the motor and a spin of the tyres, she sped away.

Leo walked back into the kitchen, grabbing a bottle of water from the fridge. Sinking onto a nearby couch, he exhaled heavily.

Bella joined him 'Sorry you had to see all that, Bella.'

Sitting next to him, a small smile curled her lips. 'Don't worry, Leo. I'm not easily scared off.'

With a wry chuckle, he muttered something about Evelyn's legendary meltdowns, but Bella cut him off gently. 'Leo, it's your birthday. Put the past in the past.' She tugged his hand. 'I feel like dancing. Come on, old man.'

'Old man? Who's an old man?' 'You, if you don't dance.'

Laughter and music filled the night as they danced to '80s and '90s hits. During a break, Chloe and Sarah dragged Leo back onto the dance floor for their usual routine. Chaotic, hilarious, and obviously well-practiced since childhood. Guests stopped to watch.

The music stopped and guests made their was to the food area. Cook appeared, presenting the chocolate sponge ablaze with sparklers.

'Couldn't fit any more sparklers on,' laughed Bill. 'Hey, cut it out, I am not over the hill yet.' Leo replied.

Leo took the first slice, then handed the second to Bella.

'Not fair!' Sarah protested.

'Did you bake me a cake?' Leo challenged.

'No.'

'Then wait your turn.'

Leo took an enormous bite to tease the girls.

Leo cut another slice, finally sharing it with the girls.

Later, Bill handed him a plastic bag with an unwrapped book inside. 'A murder mystery. Thanks, Dad.'

They danced as the band played '80s and '90s hits. Leo couldn't believe how lighthearted and carefree he felt.

'Bella, do you ever get tired?' 'Only when the music stops.'

Bella took off, quietly asking Cook to help her. They went into her room, and Cook picked up a heavy box.

'This sure is heavy. What is it?' he asked.

'Not telling. Can you sit it on the table in front of Leo, please?'

'Oh, I see another gift,' Leo called out loudly.

Bella handed him a card, and he laughed at the joke inside, passing it to Bill to read. 'What on earth is this big gift?' He tore off the wrapping and opened the box. The girls were right beside him.

'What is it?' Sarah said as she peered over Leo's shoulder.

'Fruit,' said Chloe, making a funny face.

Leo could hardly get a word out; he was bent over, laughing so hard. He caught a look at Bella, and she was giggling.

'Apples! Bloody apples!' Leo yelled. 'Bella, you devil… I am going to eat them all myself and never let the horses near them.' He circled around to where she was standing. 'Bella, that is priceless.'

Bella smirked. 'You'll have to share with the horses.'

'Never! These are mine!' he declared dramatically before pulling Bella close and kissing her on the lips.

Whistles erupted from the crowd.

Chloe elbowed Sarah. 'She's staff, right?' Sarah grinned. 'I remember her now. She was in Uncle Steve's wedding.'

'And she can cook. That cake was amazing. But does she like horses?'

Bill chuckled. 'She's a natural. How's that for a city girl?'

'Who knew?' Chloe murmured.

'No one,' Bill said. 'Not even me.'

Chapter 15

Leo and Bella cuddled close together on the couch in a quiet corner, their conversation a gentle murmur in the dim light. By 2:30 a.m., the soft hum of the empty house had settled over the party, and the last echoes of laughter faded into the night.

'Bella, this has been one of my best birthdays. Thank you,' Leo said, his voice soft with sincerity. He leaned in, his warm breath tickling her neck before his lips brushed her skin. The delicate pressure sent a shiver down her spine. As his strong arms gathered her into a tender embrace, her heartbeat steadied in rhythm with his. Every touch, every kiss deepened the unspoken knowing that she was exactly where she belonged. Leo pulled back slightly, hesitation flickering in his eyes.

'Bella, I don't want to spoil what's between us by rushing into this. I should probably head back down the hill to my place.' A playful smile tugged at Bella's lips as she nudged his arm.

'Just when I'm getting interested,' she teased, her eyes

sparkling with mischief. Grasping his hand, she added, 'I'm sleeping in a queen-sized bed.' Leo's eyebrows lifted, amusement dancing in his eyes.'

Are you sure?'

'Never been surer,' Bella replied, her voice light as she brushed her lips against his in a lingering, tender kiss.

Chapter 16

The first shaft of light crept through the window. Bella's eyelids fluttered gently rousing her from sleep. She swung her legs over the side of the bed, pulled on her tracksuit and runners, draping a warm scarf around her neck. Quietly, she closed the door behind her. Not to go for a run, but to visit Velvet Glow, who was already out on an early morning training run.

Outside, the air was cool, with pockets of mist hanging eerily close to the ground. The ground crunched underfoot with icy edges on the frosted leaves. As Bella made her way toward the white fence lining the track, she could just make out two horses at full gallop. Her heart quickened when she recognised the familiar silhouette of Velvet Glow. Leaning against the outer rail, she watched intently as the pair raced by. A delighted clap escaped when Velvet Glow passed close enough for her to be sure. A figure emerged further down the fence and made his way toward her.

'Good morning, Bill,' Bella greeted him with a warm smile. Bill's eyes crinkled in greeting.

'You're up early today, Bella.'

'I wanted to see what training you were doing with Velvet Glow,' she explained, curiosity lighting her voice. Bill nodded, his tone friendly as he described how he was pairing Velvet Glow with a retired racehorse to help her get used to galloping close to another horse. Bella peppered him with questions, her eyes bright as she absorbed every detail. Together, they leaned on the rail, intently watching each horse as the next pair began their run.

After a few laps, Bill turned to her. 'Which one do you think is the fastest?'

Without missing a beat, Bella said, 'Definitely the black one. It never shows any sign of tiredness.'

'That's Starfire,' Bill explained. 'He's a four-year-old with the will and the stamina, but we still need to build his muscle strength to go the full distance.'

Bella squinted thoughtfully. 'It's all in the little things,' she mused. 'The way they stride, or even how they kick out their feet. I noticed his back left hoof doesn't lift as high as the right one.'

Bill raised his binoculars to get a closer look. 'We can sometimes overlook the small details in favour of the big picture like diet, timing, and such. I'll have his trainer video him so we can see if you're right.'

A soft laugh escaped her. 'I'm no expert, remember. It may be my imagination.'

Chapter 17

Leo walked into the kitchen, shaking the droplets from his wet hair as he emerged from the shower. The aroma of freshly brewed coffee had him searching for a mug.

'Hell, what time did you get up, Bella?' he asked, a teasing smile tugging at his lips.

Bella's thoughts drifted back to the early light that had crept through her window, painting the walls in soft golden hues. 'The first light that came through the window woke me,' she replied, her voice warm with recollection.

She continued eagerly, 'Leo, you should have seen Velvet Glow running this morning. Her chestnut tail streamed behind her like a flag.' Her eyes sparkled with enthusiasm as she recalled the sight.

Leo chuckled. 'All horses have tails that do that, Bella not just Velvet Glow.' His eyes danced with mischief.

'I loved watching her. She has my heart,' Bella said, a subtle warmth blooming in her chest at the thought of the graceful horse.

'Good thing you don't live here. She'd be the most spoiled horse on the stud. Hope you didn't give her apples,' Leo teased, raising an eyebrow.

Bella smirked. 'I might have. But that's my secret.' Her heart

fluttered at the memory of the horse's sweet nuzzle against her palm.

Without warning, Leo pulled her into a warm embrace. His body enveloped hers as he leaned down for a kiss that sent a thrilling shiver through her. Later, with a playful glint in her eye, she recalled, 'I also saw Starfire not up close; he was training down at the track.' The sleek, black horse had captured her imagination as much as Velvet Glow had.

Inside the kitchen, Leo glanced toward Bill. 'Dad, what do you think of someone who gets up at the crack of dawn like you?' he asked, his tone light.

'Great company for coffee,' Bill grinned. Their laughter mingled with the low hum of conversation. Leo sat at the table joining Bill. They began to plot out the week's work timetable.

Meanwhile, Bella wandered around the property. Her fingers trailed along the rough wooden stalls and brushed the cool metal of the gates. She ventured into the horse stalls, her heart swelling as she patted each inquisitive head that peeked out, their warm breath whispering against her hand. Bella loved the smell of fresh hay, and the distant whinnies from the horses outside, setting the morning's tone. When Leo found her, he paused to watch as she confidently interacted with the horses. A smile tugged at the corner of his mouth. 'Ever do any riding?' he asked, curiosity bright in his eyes.

Bella hesitated, a hint of nervousness in her tone.

'Nooo! A few rides as a kid with someone handling the reins probably doesn't count as riding up here.'

'Would you like to ride with me? I'm taking the girls' horses out for some gentle exercise,' Leo suggested, his warm gaze sending her pulse racing.

'I wouldn't know what to do, and I think I'm too old to start a show-jumping career,' she laughed, though her heart fluttered at the idea.

'Both these horses are old and prefer a slow walk to a gallop,' Leo assured her, his tone gentle and reassuring.

As Leo saddled up the horses, he explained the basics with deft hands working the tack. Bella felt a surge of determination even as the prospect of riding filled her with trepidation. Standing before the imposing height of the creature, she whispered, 'I'll try it. It's scary, though, Leo.'

'Yep. I figured you'd feel that way, but I know you're very brave,' he encouraged, his words wrapping around her like a warm blanket and igniting a spark of confidence.

Together, they walked the horses down to the training ring, Bella's heart pounding with anticipation. Once inside, Leo pulled a small stool over and helped her into the saddle. The cool leather pressed against her skin, and she could feel the subtle shift of the horse's muscles beneath her.

At first, the horse moved with a gentle walk, then shifted into a slow trot. Bella gripped the reins tightly; her palms grew clammy as anxiety mingled with excitement.

'Loosen the reins a bit, Bella, and try to relax. The horse can tell if you're nervous,' Leo advised, his calm, steady voice guiding her despite the knot in her stomach.

'Mmmm, not easy I'm slipping all over this seat,' she admitted, her breath quickening as she shifted her weight.

'Saddle.' Leo hid a huge laugh that tried to escape. Use your leg muscles and knees to push into the side of the saddle; that'll stop you from sliding,' Leo said, holding back a laugh.

Concentrating hard, Bella focused on his instructions. With each rhythmic step of the horse, she began to sense the gentle pulse of its movement a quiet reminder of the trust forming between them. After half an hour, Leo called out, 'Let's do one more trot around and then head back to the stables.' His voice was encouraging, and with that final lap, Bella's confidence surged.

When Leo produced another stool to help her off the horse, she laughed. 'My bum is sore,' the thrill of the ride still dancing in her veins.

'Yep, that's horses for you,' he grinned in response.

Just then, a vehicle pulled up outside the stables. Chloe and Sarah tumbled out, their laughter ringing through the crisp morning air.

'Have you already ridden them today?' Chloe asked, her eyes sparkling with excitement.

'Just around the training track,' Leo replied with a wink. 'They're ready for you to take a ride.'

'Want to come with us, Dad?' Sarah chimed in, her enthusiasm infectious.

Leo glanced at Bella, who returned his look with a soft smile, warmth spreading through her at the thought of being included. He saddled up another horse, walked out of the stables, and gave Bella a quick kiss in passing. Then, without warning, Leo mounted his horse, called out loudly, and they took off at a gallop down the hillside.

Bella stood for a moment in shock, her heart racing, not just from the thrill of the ride but also from the sudden real-isation of the deep connection blossoming between them.

And though Leo had teased her that these old horses wouldn't gallop, the absurdity of it made her laugh. She knew then that he had tricked her into riding, but instead of feeling deceived, she felt exhilarated. The adventure had only just begun, and Bella loved every moment of it.

Chapter 18

The frosty morning had blossomed into a sunny, warm day, the sunlight casting a golden glow over the stud farm. Bella strolled along the paddock fences, her heart swelling with gratitude as she took in the picturesque scene. The rhythmic clinking of horseshoes on the cobbled paths. Riders glided smoothly on the track, while grooms meticulously washed and brushed the horses, voices mingling with the occasional whinny.

As she admired the beauty of the stud, Bella felt a wave of nostalgia wash over her. The sight of the majestic horses up close stirred something deep within her a longing for a passion she had never fully pursued. She had always loved horses from afar, but now, surrounded by their warmth and vitality, it struck her how easy it was to feel alive in their presence. Each breath she took filled her with the fresh scent of hay and leather, and she couldn't help but capture the moment, snapping photos as if to freeze this perfect day in time.

Settling onto a nearby bench, she began flicking

through the photos on her phone, her eyes sparkling with delight. 'That's a nice one of Velvet Glow,' came a voice behind her, rich and friendly. Bella turned around to find Cook, standing a few feet away with a warm smile. She's my favourite, Bella admitted, turning the screen toward him, eager to share her joy.

'Where in the family do you fit in, Cook?' she asked, her curiosity piqued. 'And what is your name? I haven't had time to find out.'

'It's Justin. Most people have forgotten it; everyone that loves me calls me Cook.'

'Not, 'The Cook'? Bella teased, raising an eyebrow.

'Nah, just Cook,' he chuckled, a twinkle in his eye.

'So, you prefer food to horses?' she asked, her tone light but genuinely intrigued.

'Yes, I do. The kitchen is my domain to do with as I please. I live in the top house with Uncle Fred.' His pride was palpable as he spoke. 'My mother and father were killed in an accident when I was ten. So, Fred adopted me, and he and Bill, mum's two brothers took me in as their son. I have total family rights just like Steve and Leo.'

'What an enormous challenge that must have been for you at ten.' Bella said with concern.

'It was, I hated it at first. I didn't want to be here. However, we got through a few years of struggling with school and career, and here I am. This is my home.' I tried to like horses, but it just wasn't in my blood. One day we had a client coming and I said I would make some scones, Fred said go for it. Well, the first batch were flat and black. The next ones were ok. But I kept trying and finally I learnt how to make them. Whenever a caterer, would come in for an event, I would be in the kitchen with them. Learning everything I could. Food fascinated me. So Fred and bill got me an apprentice ship in Melbourne with a top restaurant. I loved it and came home every weekend and cooked for the family.

' Oh what a change from horses.' Bella said.

' Yes, it was, then I went to France to a high-end restaurant and a school for a year and came out a Corden blue chef.'

Can you ride a horse at all? Bella laughed.

'Yes, I had to take lessons because Fred and Bill are big on knowing the business from the saddle up.' But I am not much of a rider, and it's not a hobby of mine.' I don't love horses like you do; you are a natural horse lover.'

'Yes I am.' Bella smiled and realised just how kind Justin was. As they continued chatting about the stud and the horses, Bella noticed the warmth in Justin's gaze. Then he turned serious, his tone taking on a deeper note.

'Bella, I really hope you are serious about Leo. He has had a shattering life with Evelyn. He has been crushed. His girls and horses are his life.'

Bella laughed, her voice light but her heart a little heavy. 'Is everyone here protective of Leo?'

'Yes. We have all been through enough of Evelyn and her psycho fighting to last a lifetime.'

'Well, it's so lovely that you care this much about Leo,' she said, raising her head to meet Justin's eyes, her sincerity shining through. 'What if I say no, not interested?'

Holding her gaze, Justin replied earnestly, 'I would talk really hard to get you to go home.' Bella laughed, the sound brightening the air around them.

'Well, I had better not put a foot wrong around you then. Leo is one of the most genuine guys I have ever met, Justin. Truly, he is such a gentleman.'

Relief washed over Justin's face, and they continued

scrolling through the photos, the camaraderie between them deepening.

'We are all hoping you are exactly what he needs, and I am pretty sure you are,' he added, his voice warm.

'Well, that's reassuring, knowing I have passed the taste test by the Cook.' Bella smiled, feeling a sense of belonging.

Just then, the sound of hooves clopping against the dirt alerted them to Leo and the girls returning from their ride. Bella and Justin walked down to the stables, anticipation buzzing in the air. 'Nice ride?' Bella called out as they approached.

'Super, and I won!' Sarah chimed, her face flushed with excitement.

'No, you didn't! You didn't even go around the tree. You turned back before the end!'

Leo laughed, his voice carrying across the paddock. 'Little cheat,' he added playfully. 'I'm the real winner.'

'No, you weren't, Dad. You were last into the stable!' Chloe yelled her laughter ringing like music. The atmosphere was thick with humour and banter as Bella stood by the stalls, absorbing their cheerful interaction.

'Hey Bella, who do you think won?' Leo asked, a mischievous glint in his eye. Bella put both her hands on her hips, jutting her chin defiantly.

'Definitely Leo.'

'Why?' both girls shouted in unison, feigning indignation. 'Don't be on his side!'

'Girls, did you know you two are miracle workers?' Bella said calmly, her smile widening.

Chloe tilted her head, a slight frown forming. 'Oh no, she's not a religious nut, is she, Dad?'

'However, neither of those horses could gallop an hour ago. They could only walk slowly around the arena because they are so old.' Chloe shook her head, her eyes wide with disbelief.

' What?' Both girls turned to look at their father. 'Leo was roaring with laughter, trying to hide behind his horse.'

'Dad, what did you tell Bella to get her onto a horse?' Chloe demanded, half-laughing, half-annoyed.

'Don't worry, girls, I'll get back at him.' Bella said playfully. It was a fun time as the girls began wiping down and brushing the horses. 'Can I help?' Bella asked eagerly. 'Of course,' they replied, their excitement infectious.

'Maybe we can help you get back at Dad,' Sarah suggested with a conspiratorial grin.

'No, you don't, girls. Bella is quite capable of getting in the game with me,' Leo said, his voice teasing. Bella brushed one side of the horse while Chloe brushed the other, the rhythm of their movements creating a sense of camaraderie.

'What do I do with his mane, Chloe?' asked Bella, her brow furrowed in concentration.

'Gee, I thought you knew a lot about horses,' Chloe teased lightly. 'Nope, just had my first ride today, on a horse that was too old to gallop.' Bella chuckled, the joy of the day spilling over into her words. The girls erupted into laughter.

'Dad is such a tease,' Sarah said, shaking her head.

'Never,' he replied with mock indignation. Cook, watching from the sidelines, felt a sense of peace settle over him. He observed the natural ease with which Bella interacted with the girls and Leo, feeling more confident in his belief that she would suit Leo perfectly.

' Morning, all! a voice called out, and Uncle Fred approached, arms outstretched for hugs. The girls rushed to greet him, their chatter mixing with the sounds of the farm.

'Sarah cheated' said Chloe.

'I'm sure she didn't. We don't have any cheats in this family, he laughed, ruffling their hair.

'Not fair. Don't stick up for her,' Leo said, shaking his head. 'She didn't round the tree before turning for home.'

'Smart kid, I'd say,' Fred replied with a chuckle, walking toward Bella with an outstretched hand.

'Hello, Bella, nice to see you again.' Bella remembered him from the wedding, Steve's dad, his presence warm and inviting.

'Bella, I hear a rumour that you are attached to my nephew,' Fred said, his tone teasing.

'Uncle Fred, you don't know the half of it,' Chloe spoke excitedly 'Dad made Bella ride a very old horse that couldn't gallop anymore. He took her around the arena a few times.'

'Oh, Leo, not that old one… and which horse was it, Bella?' Fred inquired, curiosity shining in his eyes as she pointed to the one she was brushing.

'Yes, this one,' Bella added, grinning. 'It was old and decrepit one minute, and the next it was galloping down the paddocks.' Fred smiled, amusement dancing in his eyes. 'You haven't ridden much, I take it, Bella?'

'Not at all,' she smiled, her heart light as she embraced the companionship of the moment.

Chapter 19

There was a small group left over from the party who had stayed for the weekend. Leo had invited everyone to his house for a swim, spa, and BBQ.

Bella joined Leo in the kitchen and began helping him with the food. 'You're a guest, Bella you don't have to do any cooking,' he teased.

'I don't mind,' she replied with a soft smile as she started mixing the marinade for the meat and tossing together a Caesar salad. 'Where did you learn to cook?' Bella asked.

'We all learn a bit of everything on the stud,' Leo explained.

'Bill always says that since we all love eating, we better be able to cook. I started early, and I love getting into the kitchen though not every day.'

'Do you clean up afterward?' he prodded.

'Yep, I'm a neat freak.'

'Me too.' Leo grinned.

'Did you bring your bathers, Bella?'

'No, I didn't know there'd be swimming,' she admitted.

'Okay, we have a rack of spares in the hall cupboard. Try and find a pair that fits.' Bella found the bathers neatly hung in the cupboard and tried on a floral pink pair. 'How do these look, Leo?'

'Wow with a capital W. Bella, you'd look amazing in anything,' he said, wiping his hands on a towel before pulling her into a warm hug. 'Thank you for coming up for my birthday, Bella. You've made this weekend perfect for me. How about you?'

'Leo, it's been years since I've had this much fun. I love your company,' she replied, her eyes lighting up. Leo kissed Bella sweetly, and she returned his kiss with genuine gratitude.

'Thank you,' she whispered.

'What for?' Leo teased. 'The salad isn't finished yet.'

Bella moved behind him and wrapped her arms around his waist. 'Thank you for being you,' she murmured, feeling the comforting warmth of his body.

'Why don't you try the pool? It's heated, and once I'm done here, I'll join you.'

Before long, Bella was doing laps in the pool when Leo suddenly jumped in, sending a splash that sparked a playful water fight between them. Soon, the girls joined in, and it turned into a full-blown water war.

'Bella, you have the best hair,' Chloe called out as she swam by. 'It stays curly and looks great, wet or dry.'

'I'm just lucky, I guess,' Bella laughed. A few friends joined the chatter and splashes.

'Oh no,' the girls exclaimed in unison.

'What's up?' Leo asked.

'You do not want to know,' Chloe replied with a serious tone. Then, the loud bang of a car door slamming shut cut through the pool noise. Through the double doors strode Evelyn.

'Hi, Mum,' the girls chorused. 'Bit cold for swimming, isn't it?' Evelyn remarked, surveying the scene.

'It's heated, Mum it's really warm,' Sarah countered. Evelyn's eyes swept the pool area, nodding to a few she recognised. Then she stopped. Fixating on Bella. Her voice rang out, loud and demanding: 'And who might you be?'

'Mum, this is Bella,' Chloe interjected.

'Bella who? Leo hasn't introduced us. Are you new on staff?' Evelyn bellowed.

Leo's eyes darkened, and he shook his head. 'Not again,' he muttered under his breath.

'Evelyn, why are you here?' Leo asked quietly.

'Well, since I wasn't invited to your party, I thought I'd come and collect the girls to drive them home,' she snapped.

'It's okay, Mum we're not going home today. We're leaving tomorrow. Dad is driving us down,' Sarah replied, trying to keep her tone even.

'No. I made the effort to pick you up. Get your things together,' Evelyn insisted, her tone rising.

Leo edged to the side of the pool and swung out.

'Tomorrow. They're going home tomorrow,' Leo said firmly. 'They're not children; they're adults who don't need you to organise them anymore.'

Evelyn got close to Leo and yelled in his face. 'I am driving them home. Today. You are a useless man. I have had to do everything for the girls. You idiot, Leo. Don't try to stop me. I am taking the girl's home. NOW.'

Bella got out of the pool at the shallow end and walked up to where Evelyn was standing at the side of the pool as she berated Leo. 'Nice to meet you, Evelyn. I'm Bella.'

'What, what have you got on? Those are my bathers. I haven't worn them for years.' Evelyn's voice was now shrill as she stared at Bella.

'Too small for you, are they?' Bella said quietly.

'No,' she spat at Bella. 'So, you are who is staying in the house.' Bella didn't flinch. 'Evelyn, you look like a nice person, but what is coming out of your mouth tells me that you are a vindictive bitch. Why are you so nasty to a person you have just met?'

'What did you call me?' Bella turned to go inside. 'Excuse me,' she said.

'Get my bathers off. Get them off now.'

Bella stopped. She slowly turned and walked back to face Evelyn. 'Now?' said Bella.

'They are mine,' Evelyn screamed.

Without hesitation, Bella slipped her arms out of the straps of the bathers, grabbed Leo's towel from a nearby chair, and pulled the bathers off. She walked over and pushed them into Evelyn's hands. 'Well,' Evelyn said icily, 'you could apologise for wearing my bathers.'

At that moment, two cars pulled up outside. Bill and Fred emerged through the door. 'Evelyn, why are you here?' Bill demanded. 'This… this person is wearing my bathers!' Evelyn screamed.

Before Bill and Fred could reach her, Bella gave Evelyn a short, sharp push. 'Enjoy your swim,' Bella said coolly as she walked away.

Furious, Evelyn fell into the pool fully clothed, making a huge splash. The girls laughed as the other guests dispersed. Bill and Fred quickly grabbed Evelyn's arms and hauled her out of the pool. She was dripping wet and mortified.

'She… she pushed me into the pool!' Evelyn screamed. 'There is nothing of yours left here, Evelyn,' Leo declared, his voice rising. 'Nothing!' He repeated, louder this time. His body began to shake visibly with distress. Fred and Bill wrapped a towel around Evelyn and led her inside.

'Evelyn, we've called the police,' Bill said. 'You are not welcome here again.'

'Good I can tell the police a woman pushed me into the pool and stole my bathers,' Evelyn muttered

'No,' Bill replied firmly. 'You had your bathers in your hand a minute ago. Are they still in the pool? We now have an order barring you from our property.' The next car to pull up was Janet, Evelyn's sister. As she entered the lounge, seeing Evelyn sopping wet, she burst into laughter. Spotting Bella, she quickly pieced things together.

'Oh, I see, Leo,' she said. 'Okay, let's get Evelyn back to my place.'

'I want my bathers,' Evelyn insisted. Sarah and Chloe dove to the bottom of the pool and retrieved them.

'I don't think you've ever worn them, Mum. Are you even sure they're yours?' Sarah teased as she handed the wet bathers back to her.

'Yes, they're mine,' Evelyn insisted. Fred and Bill escorted Evelyn into her sister's car. Bill drove her car while Fred took his own to drive Bill back from Janet's place.

Bella had swapped her towel for dry clothes and walked around searching for Leo. She found him in the lounge, head in his hands, rocking slightly back and forth.

'Bella, I wanted to laugh about you pushing Evelyn into the pool, but I'm... I'm overwhelmed by all this pressure,' Leo confessed, his voice trembling. Bella sat beside him on the arm of the chair and gently held his hand. Leo's face was pale his words jumbled and incoherent. Bella reached out and caressed his cheek, offering silent comfort even as his shaking worsened. Leo burst into tears. The shock hit

Bella hard. She put her arm around his shoulders, trying to steady him. Bella wasn't accustom to the sensitivity of mental illness, and she didn't know what else to do. She barely noticed the sound of a car pulling up outside until she saw Cook racing into the room. Leaning over, he wrapped his arms around Leo.

Bella stepped back and settled onto the couch as Cook spoke urgently. 'Bella, could you get some brandy from the kitchen cupboard, a teaspoon, and some water. Leo's in deep shock.' Bella moved quickly, retrieving the brandy and a teaspoon, 'he hates the stuff, but it should give him a little jolt.

Here we go, Leo just take this,' Cook said, holding the teaspoon up to Leo's mouth. Leo swallowed the small measure of brandy, screwing up his nose at the taste. Leo remained unresponsive shaking, crying, his words a jumble.

'Okay,' Cook said, 'help me get him into the car.' 'He's still wet from the pool,' Bella replied. 'I'll grab some clothes and a towel.' They carefully helped Leo into the back of the car, and Bella climbed into the seat beside him. Leo collapsed, resting his head in her lap. Bella's heart pounded with fear for him. She felt a small relief when Chloe jumped into the other side to take over as nurse, and Sarah sat in the front seat.

'Hospital,' Chloe declared. 'We'll be faster than an ambulance.' As they drove, they dried Leo off and draped a wind cheater over him. A dry towel was placed over his legs to warm him. Meanwhile, Cook spoke urgently on the phone, arranging for an ambulance to meet them on the main road in twelve minutes. Sarah shed quiet tears as she sat in the front. Bella held Leo's hand and tried to do anything that would make him comfortable.

They met the ambulance and transferred Leo into the

back. The paramedics inserted an IV and administered a sedative. Within minutes, Leo was asleep.

'No extra passengers,' said the ambulance driver. 'We've taken Leo before; we will look after him.' Cook shut the doors of the ambulance and walked back to the car.

'I'll go in later and take clothes for him.' Bella and the girls were all silent on the drive back up the mountain. There was nothing they could think of to say. Each one was hurting for Leo in their own way

Chapter 20

By the time they got back to the house the guests had started the barbecue and set up the food. Cook went in and let them know the ambulance was taking Leo to hospital.

'I think he will be in for a couple of days,' he said. 'It usually takes that long to get over a bad panic attack.'

Two lots of Evelyn in two days brings it all up again. Cook looked for Bella and decided to fill her in on Leo's health. She was in the lounge room on the couch. He sat next to her and looked at her with a very serious face.

'This is not a new situation Bella, and I need to explain to you why Leo collapsed. I hope you will understand.

'Bella, Leo has C-PTSD it is a psychological trauma response from being battered down emotionally by Evelyn. She has a very unfortunate personality, once she has an idea in her head she will not stop until she gets every detail. Evelyn has yelled and accused Leo for years over any minor thing she could think of. While she lived here it seemed that not only Leo got her wrath, but anyone who was his friend got it as well. It has been a serious concern for the family for years. After many determined tries Bill and Fred insisted, she and Leo have counselling. Finally, she was diagnosed with narcissist tendency.'

'It was quiet for a time then she refused to go to the counselling sessions and she became more and more difficult to manage. Eventually she agreed to the divorce terms, and went to Melbourne to live. The girls were there through the week and here nearly every weekend. They were much happier with the split living.' Bella listened, as many confusing thoughts ran through her mind. 'Thanks Cook for explaining this to me, what a dreadful thing to live through. I feel so helpless, that there was nothing I could do for Leo.'

As Fred and Bill returned from delivering Evelyn to her sister's house, they came into the lounge room. Cook had made fresh coffee.

'How are you Bella? 'I am fine Bill, but truly jolted at such a harmful person.'

'I wasn't joking about getting an order out on Evelyn. Our solicitor has started the process. If she comes here again, we just call the police immediately,' said Bill.

Bella shook her head. 'It's drastic measure to have to take, isn't it.' Fred nodded and Bill shook his head in agreement. She knew by their actions that it wasn't something they would do without a lot of thought. Cook filled them in with all the details. 'I am so sorry Bella it's scary to see Leo in a full on panic attack. His mental ordeal only started when he was with Evelyn. She is a hard hearted woman.'

'I am so upset for Leo, will he be, ok? and get the right care? Where are they taking him?'

'Yes Bella, he is getting the right care, Cook will visit him tomorrow morning at the hospital, and let us know how he is. Hopefully, by then he will be settled down.' Bill explained. Bella felt tears rundown her cheeks, she couldn't stop crying.

'Oh, Justin this is awful, he is the kindest person I know.'

'Yes.' said Justin quietly.' 'It's been a huge weekend for him and he didn't pace himself enough. Then Evelyn turning up twice pushed him over the edge. 'Not to mention that Bella tried to drown her,' laughed Cook.' Leo's going to get miles out of that one.'

Bella could not laugh, she wondered if she had made it worse. Probably it did but it was a spontaneous reaction.

'It will be really important for Leo to see you when he comes home Bella will you stay on until he is better,' asked Bill.

'Of course.'

Cook rang Bella late the next day and said that he will be bringing Leo home in the morning. 'Bella you are all he wants to see. He is worried that this might complicate your friendship. So I have told him you are still here.'

Bella wiped her eyes, 'Where else would I be I am so worried about him.'

'Thanks Bella.' said Cook.

Bella tossed and turned all night going over the whole birthday weekend. Chloe and Sarah had decided to stay on for a week. Sarah was up early helping with the horses and contemplating when would be a good time to ask the family if she could live at the stud and become a trainer? She would like to tell Leo first so he had some good news to come home too.

Bill guessed the reason Sarah was deciding on a different career, and approached her. 'Think hard about your decision Sarah, we would welcome you with open arms, but two things have to fall into place first. Are you prepared to commit to the long years of training, and go through all the same steps that all new employees have to go through. You know how we run the stud, everyone is equal. We know you have the talent to become a trainer, and where better to do it than here with us. So, think deeply if you really want this lifestyle.'

'I have been tossing it up for two years Grandpa, University is not for me, I really don't like the course I am doing. I have been through all the courses open to me, and all I want to do is to be home with all the horses and you. There is nothing I love better than working with horses.'

'Let's talk it over with your Dad when he gets home. You know he will say yes immediately. He would love to have you close.'

'Then there is your mother, we will have to talk in depth about her visiting you. We won't tolerate her visiting the stud. So I'm glad you are staying the week so we can sort this out.'

'Have you talked it over with Chloe?' Fred enquired. 'Yes, she thinks my heart lies with horses and she encourages me to talk with you and Grand Pa.'

Bella was sitting on the front veranda when cook's car drove in. She didn't rush to the car she waited until Leo and cook got out. Leo looked pale and withdrawn. Bella walked to him and gave him a kiss on the cheek, he put his hand out to clasp her, and they hugged. She could feel his weakness, as they walked inside. Cook made coffee as they relaxed in the lounge room. Leo looked up at Bella and started to talk.

'Bella I...' She cuddled into him and said, 'let's talk later Leo. I'm not going anywhere.' He sat on the couch and Bella sat next to him. 'Once you feel more awake, we'll take you for a walk outside.' 'What do you feel like eating Leo?' asked Cook.

'Something light.' Cook went off to make Leo an omelet, leaving him with Bella. Leo woke late in the afternoon and came out to find Bella. She hugged him close and walked with him to the lounge room. As they sat on the couch Bella looked at Leo's pale face. His energy was depleted even though he had had plenty of sleep.

'Bella I thought I might lose you once you knew how deeply my nervous system is stuffed.'

'Sorry to disappoint you Leo, I'm still here.' Bella smiled at Leo and kissed his cheek. 'I'm not going anywhere until I have had another ride on one of those old non galloping horses you so proudly introduced me too.'

Leo managed a half smile, and cuddled Bella tight. 'Where are the girls?' In their rooms, they are staying for the week to keep you company.

'Are you talking about us?' Sarah said as the sisters walked into the room. 'Dad how do you feel?' 'A bit weak and tired.' 'What do you feel like eating? We'll make it for you.'

'Coffee.' said Leo. 'Bella, coffee?' asked Sarah ? Yes, no sugar Leo lay his head back against the back of the couch, his eyes half closed, 'where is everybody?'

'All up at the top house. I'm sure Grand Pa and Uncle Fred will be happy to know you are awake, and home.' Said Bella. 'Justin's been caring for you.'

'So, it's Justin now! Mumbled Leo, should I be worried.'

'Depends how many horses he has to offer.'

'Not a horseman,' whispered Leo. It was easy for Bella to sit quietly with Leo, no pressure to talk, just the comfort of his presence. She held his hand, feeling the warmth of it, grounding herself in the moment. The coffee arrived, and

Sarah and Chloe joined them. Leo had drifted back to sleep, his breathing slow and steady. The girls and Bella sat in companionable silence. Cook entered with a tray piled high with sandwiches.

'Enough for an army,' Sarah joked as he walked in. Cook chuckled. 'Not all for you two.' He set the tray down and took a seat, turning his attention to Bella.

'Leo will be in and out of sleep for the next 24 hours. Every time he wakes up, try to get him to drink something and eat a little.'

'I will,' Bella promised.

'Girls, help Bella out if she needs a break during the night.'

Chloe raised an eyebrow. 'Trying to be Dad now, Cook?'

'Yep. And if I were, you two wouldn't be so spoiled,' he teased. The laughter was light, but the weight of the past few days still lingered. Bella excused herself, needing a moment alone. She wandered outside, letting the cool evening air clear her mind. Her feet carried her to the paddock near the house. Velvet Glow stood by the fence, her dark eyes watching as Bella approached. The mare stepped closer, lowering her head as Bella reached out, running a hand over the soft curve of her face. A wave of emotion hit. Relief, exhaustion, gratitude. Tears slipped down Bella's cheeks, but this time, they weren't from fear. Velvet Glow nudged her gently before dropping her head to graze on the long, lush grass by the fence. Bella inhaled deeply, grounding herself in the steady presence of the horse. She had always found peace with them, and right now, she needed it more than ever.

Chapter 21

Bella needed time alone to sort through the storm of thoughts swirling in her mind. Every time she looked at Leo, her heart affirmed with quiet certainty he was the one. Yet beneath that certainty lay a tremor of fear. Could she truly care for him when his mind slipped into those unsettling breakdowns? She had no personal experience with mental illness, but she resolved to change that. She would seek guidance from a doctor or psychologist, determined to learn how to support him in the best way possible.

That evening, Bella wandered the stud grounds, her gaze fixed on the darkening sky as the last of the sunlight melted below the horizon. The quiet majesty of dusk stirred something deep inside her a fragile mix of hope and apprehension, mirroring the turmoil in her heart.

Inside, the girls took turns keeping vigil over Leo. He slept fitfully, slipping into brief, troubled slumbers lasting only a few hours at a time, waking just long enough to mumble or pace the room.

Though Bella managed short rests between their

watchful shifts, she refused to fully sleep. Anxiety kept her alert, listening for any sign of distress.

At first light, Cook arrived to check on Leo. In the lounge, Bella dozed lightly on the couch, the girls curled up beside their father. She stirred as Cook entered the room.

How's he doing?' he asked, his voice low. Bella rubbed her eyes. 'Restless. Wakes every few hours, talking in his sleep.'The worry in her tone was unmistakable.

Cook nodded, then gently woke the girls. 'Go to your own beds, get some real sleep. I'll stay with him until he stirs.'

Two hours later, Leo's eyelids fluttered open. He blinked at the sight of Cook in the chair beside his bed and managed a weak smile.

'You been there all night?' he asked, voice raspy. Cook grinned. 'Nah, just about an hour. The girls watched you all night they've gone to bed, and Bella's on the couch in the lounge. No idea what you've done to earn all this attention.' Leo chuckled, shaking his head.

'Go have a shower,' Cook said. 'I'll make you some breakfast.' Later, in the kitchen, Bella followed the smell of fresh coffee, her lips curving into a small smile. 'Do I smell coffee, or am I dreaming?'

Cook glanced up from the stove. 'Leo's under the shower. I think we should have a really quiet day with him.'He studied her tired expression. 'Why don't you get some sleep now that the girls are resting?'

Bella cradled her coffee cup, the warmth doing little to ease the exhaustion weighing her down. 'I'll stay up with Leo for a while then I might crash.'

As the day unfolded, Leo grew brighter, his conversation more animated. The three of them, Bella, Leo, and Cook sat on the veranda, sharing breakfast and chatting about the stud and the horses. It was a glimpse of normalcy amid the undercurrent of tension. But as soon as Cook noticed Leo's energy flagging, he steered him inside. 'Come on, mate,' Cook said. 'Let's catch up on some horse racing videos.'

Leo barely made it through one race before his eyelids drooped, and he drifted into sleep on the couch.

By midweek, Leo had improved enough to attend a follow-up session with his psychologist. Bella sat beside him, pressing for advice.

'Really, there's nothing you can do that you haven't already tried,' the psychologist said gently. 'If Leo experiences another episode, it will likely be triggered by a painful interaction with his ex-wife or a sudden shock. We've put him on a mild antidepressant for a few weeks, then we'll taper it off. It's not in Leo's nature to be depressed, so we know this was a trigger response. With time and support, he'll improve.'

Walking out of the appointment, Bella felt lighter, more confident. The uncertainty that had gnawed at her was fading. She now understood, just as Cook had always been there for Leo, she would be too. There was nothing she wouldn't do to keep him safe. Bella knew she loved Leo deeply.

Chapter 22

Leo blinked slowly, his eyes half-lidded as Chloe kissed his cheek. A faint smile ghosted across his lips, though his gaze drifted, unfocused. He lifted a hand to ruffle her hair, but it dropped back to his lap before it reached its mark.

'Sit here Chloe,' Bella said, rising to her feet. She understood that both Leo and the girls needed time together, so she smiled at them before slipping into the kitchen to help Justin.

'It'll take a couple of days for Leo to get back into his normal routine,' Justin said softly, pouring a fresh cup of coffee. 'All we can do is be with him, keep things calm.'

'Alright. Just let me know what I can do,' Bella replied, glancing back toward the living room. A pang of worry tightened her chest as she saw Leo slumped in his chair, exhaustion pressing down on him. But she forced herself to focus on helping Justin.

Justin caught her expression and offered a reassuring nod. 'I'm glad Bill and Fred finally pushed ahead with legal action to keep Evelyn off the property,' he murmured.

Bella exhaled, relief mixing with disbelief. 'What a drastic step… but having met her, I can see why.' Her voice was firm, though a chill lingered in her chest at the memory of Evelyn's cold, calculating nature.

'Unhinged, unfortunately,' Cook said with a sigh. 'People tend to think of abuse as a male domain, but Evelyn proved otherwise and Leo's a marshmallow. That kind of emotional battering… it's hard to heal from.'

Fred and Bill arrived a short while later to check on Leo. They made their way into the lounge to sit with the girls, while Bella followed with a tray of coffee and cold drinks. As she set the tray down, she noticed Leo's fingers trembling slightly as he reached for his cup. A tightness gripped her chest he hadn't just survived; he'd endured. Each argument, each cruel word Evelyn had thrown at him had chipped away at something vital inside him.

'So, Cook has you working as a waitress now, Bella?' Bill teased as she handed him a cup. 'I only do it for the tips,' she replied, managing a smile. But her gaze flickered back to Leo, his weary expression a stark reminder of how fragile he still was. Bill seemed to sense the shift and spoke up.

'The order was processed yesterday, Leo. Evelyn's officially on notice not to trespass here again,' he said evenly. 'Now, we just need to work out the best way for the girls to see her so there's no mix-ups.'

'I can meet her in Melbourne for lunch or a weekend visit,' Chloe offered. Sarah nodded. 'I can go to her house sometimes. That should work, right?' Bill nodded approvingly. 'Good plan. Just make sure everything's arranged in advance. Evelyn's interpretation of things tends to… *shift*.'

A pause settled over the room before Sarah took a breath and straightened. 'Actually, I want to have a conversation with you about me being a trainer. Staying here to be trained. I know it's a big step, but I've thought about it for a long time. Grand Pa.'

Bill studied her thoughtfully. 'I hope this isn't just because of Leo,' he said gently. 'Because that alone wouldn't be enough. He'll recover.' Sarah met his gaze without hesitation. 'It's not, Grandpa. I've been thinking about this for a year. Ask Chloe.'

'Yep,' Chloe confirmed. 'She has.' 'We'll have a serious talk in a few days,' Bill said, glancing toward Leo, who had managed a weak thumbs-up before his head drooped again, exhaustion pulling at him.

'Maybe you should lie down, mate,' Justin suggested, helping him to his feet and leading him toward his room. As Bill and Bella stepped outside, Bill turned to her, his expression unreadable. 'How are you holding up, Bella? Is this all… too much?'

Bella hesitated, glancing back toward the house, toward Leo resting inside. 'Not too much,' she said finally. 'I haven't had experience with trauma or abuse, and it shocks me how deeply it's affected him, but…' her voice trailed off as she struggled to find the right words.

'It's not weakness,' Bill said quietly, reading her hesitation. 'It's years of emotional damage, each argument trapping him a little tighter, wearing him down until he didn't even see it happening.' Bella nodded, blinking back the sting of tears. 'I want to help him Bill. I know there's a lot I still have to learn, but he has my heart.'

Bill's expression softened, a rare smile touching his lips. 'By the way, the trainer of Starfire said you were astute. They watched the video of his run, and spotted his leg just in time. Turns out, he has a pulled tendon. We're resting him now to let the inflammation settle.'

'Astute!' Bella laughed, surprised. 'I've never been called that before.' A warm flicker of pride flashed across her face.

Chapter 23

'Come on, Leo,' Bella said, giving his arm a gentle tug. 'Let's visit the horses. I haven't seen Danger Man all week. Poor guy's probably wondering if I've forgotten him.'

Leo chuckled, a glint of amusement lighting his eyes. 'He's got a full schedule of pampering, Bella. Trust me he's not the one who's been missing someone.'

She laughed and gave a mock pout. 'Fine. I admit it I've missed him. You've been stealing all my time.'

'Not a bad thing,' he murmured, his gaze lingering on her face. The tiredness that had clouded his features in the hospital was gone, replaced with a calm energy she hadn't seen in weeks. As they strolled, holding hands, Bella glanced at Leo's face. He looked like himself again. B

Leo's voice shifted, quiet and thoughtful. 'I'm taking the girls home tomorrow. You coming along for the drive?' Bella offered a soft smile. 'You can drop me off at my place too.'

He bumped her shoulder gently. 'You're joking, right? I'm not letting you out of my sight.'

'Good,' she said, looping her arm through his. 'Because I'm not ready to let you go either.'

———

THEY STOPPED in front of her apartment complex. Bella unlocked the door to her unit and stepped inside. The familiar scent of lavender greeted her, but the space itself suddenly felt... small. Contained.

'Cute place,' Chloe said behind her, glancing around with an easy smile.

Bella ran her fingers along the arm of the couch. She showed the girls through, 'this is my little home she laughed, seems small after being at the stud.'

Leo hugged her at the door, pressing a kiss to her forehead. 'I'll be back in a couple of hours,' he murmured. She smiled, watching him disappear towards his car with his daughters flanking him.

———

IN THE HEART of the city, Leo found a spot in a parking garage on Collins Street. He turned to the girls as they stepped out.

'Alright, team, let's find that fancy jeweller. I most definitely need your help.' Sarah grinned and slipped her arm through his. 'Good thing we've got better taste than you, Dad.'

'Sure, Dad,' Chloe snorted, exchanging a look with Sarah.

'Good afternoon, looking for something special today? The Jeweller asked.

'Just show me some diamond rings Leo said proudly. 'I'll know it when I see it.' Chloe rolled her eyes.

'Sure, Dad. Because that's how it works.' Both girls had a giggle, and then Chloe turned to the jeweller, her tone crisp and confident. 'This is our dad, we're looking for an engagement ring. Something classic, with a diamond. Not too flashy.' The jeweller nodded and brought out two black velvet trays, the stones catching the light and throwing it in all directions.

'Remember,' Leo said, narrowing his eyes in mock warning. 'This is for Bella. Not you two.'

'Tragic,' Sarah said with a sigh, feigning disappointment. The jeweller, amused, turned to Leo. 'What's she like?' A quiet smile curved Leo's lips.

'Tall, curly hair with a bit of wild to it. Dark eyes. And a smile that… well, it knocks you sideways.'

'He's not wrong,' Sarah added. 'Bella is really beautiful.'

'Subtle, timeless style,' Chloe said. 'Not trendy. She wears pieces with meaning.'

'Ok' said the jeweller, pulling out another tray. Let's also look at this tray as well.' After looking at several rings, one caught their eye. Chloe tried it on and held out her hand under the lights.

'It looks like Bella,' Leo said softly. The jeweller nodded. 'Nice choice. That's a 1.5 carat round brilliant cut diamond on a platinum band. Sixty facets, plenty of shine. Elegant but restrained. It's the classic engagement ring.'

'It's perfect,' Sarah agreed. Chloe passed the ring back with a grin. 'You got lucky, Dad. We all love that one.' With the small box tucked securely in his pocket, Leo drove the girls toward their mother's house. The city rolled by in a blur of lights and trees, but his mind was on the box, and Bella.

As they parked outside their mother's house, he paused, turning to face the girls. 'Before you go,' he said, voice low, 'I just want to say thank you. For everything this week. And I need to know... are you okay with Bella being in our lives? I mean really okay?'

Chloe lifted a brow, amused. 'A bit late to ask, seeing as you've just bought the ring.' Leo laughed, but the question lingered in his eyes. 'She's perfect for you, Dad,' Sarah said gently.

Chloe nodded. 'She's lovely. Just… don't mess it up.'

Leo stepped out and pulled their bags from the trunk, then wrapped them both in a tight hug. 'I love you both,' he said, his voice thick. 'This next chapter, with Bella, it's going to be a good one. I can feel it.

Chapter 24

Bella had made her way through the stables to say hello to the horses. A chestnut mare poked her head over the stall door, her dark eyes soft and curious. Bella's heart lifted as she reached out, her fingers brushing the mare's velvety muzzle. The steady rise and fall of the mare's breath matched Bella's own, a quiet rhythm that calmed her as she traced the warm, silky fur along the horse's muzzle. 'Hello, beautiful,' she whispered, her voice barely more than a breath.

Inside, the stable buzzed with its usual morning rhythm. The clatter of hooves, the murmur of voices, the steady rhythm of brushes against coats. Spotting a groom working nearby, Bella approached with a smile. 'Mind if I help brush her?' she asked, nodding toward the horse.

The groom returned her smile. 'Of course not, brush's are on the shelf there she posted.' Bella had just begun brushing the horse, losing herself in the soothing strokes, when a familiar voice broke through the stable's hum.

'What are you doing, Bella?' She turned to find Leo standing watching her, his eyes bright with mischief.

'Having fun with this beauty,' she replied, patting the horse's flank.

'Come with me. I want to show you something.'

She set the brush down, curiosity sparking in her chest. 'Okay.'

As she approached, Leo reached for her hand, his grip warm and familiar. 'Let's walk up to the house paddock. I want to check on Danger Man, make sure he's in perfect shape before Steve comes home.'

They strolled side by side, the crunch of gravel beneath their feet blending with the distant rustle of leaves. Bella stole glances at Leo, the healthy glow of his cheeks, the brightness in his smile, as radiant as the day they'd met at the wedding. A quiet joy settled in her chest, blooming with every step.

'I'm so happy you're looking well, Leo,' she said softly. He squeezed her hand gently.

'It's because I have the best nurse in the world.' Bella laughed, the sound light and easy.

'Heavens, that's a lot to live up to. Really? The best in the world? How many nurses have you had?'

'None but you, and that's all I need.'

He stopped suddenly, turning to face her. Before she could react, his lips met hers in a soft, lingering kiss. When they pulled apart, Bella's heart was a wild drum in her chest.

They reached the paddock, and Danger Man's head shot up, his ears pricked toward them. Bella grinned, but her attention quickly shifted.

'Oh, look! There's Velvet Glow. Why is she in this paddock

'Oh? What's that?'

'Look over there.' He nodded toward the far side of the paddock. Bella followed his gaze and blinked in surprise. A picnic blanket lay spread beneath the shade of a large gum tree, a wicker basket perched in the middle.

'Wow,' she breathed. 'What's the occasion?'

'I wanted to thank you properly for taking such good care of me through that terrible episode.' Bella's heart softened. Leo had already thanked her countless times, but she hadn't done it for gratitude. She had cared for him simply because she wanted to.

'I wasn't looking for praise Leo.' Bella replied.

'I know.' His voice was low, sincere. 'and I'm grateful.'

They settled onto the blanket, and Leo pulled out two glasses and a bottle of champagne, placing them next to the basket. Bella's eyes widened as she read the label. 'Veuve Clicquot? That's very special.'

Leo chuckled, 'Yes, it is.' As Bella looked at Leo, his eyes grew serious. He kissed her on the forehead and stood up, reaching into his pocket. When he pulled out a small box and knelt in front of her, Bella gawked at him.

'Leo… what are you doing?' She let out a breathless laugh.

'Bella,' he said, his voice steady despite the emotion shimmering in his eyes. 'I love you with all my heart. Will you marry me?'

Pressure built behind her eyes, and before she could blink, warm tears slipped down her cheeks. She looked up at his handsome face. 'Yes,' she whispered, her voice quivering with emotion. 'Yes.'

Leo flipped open the box, revealing the diamond ring. Bella's hands shook as she felt the velvet covering of the box.

'This is a diamond, Leo,' she uttered in awe.

'Yes.'

'It's so beautiful.' Her voice broke, and more tears slipped down her cheeks. Leo reached out, brushing them away with gentle fingers.

'Bella, you're crying?' She nodded, her lips quivering. 'Yep. This is almost too much. This beautiful place, you, and both horses I love are here.'

Leo sat down beside her, pulling her into his arms. 'Come on,' he murmured, 'let's see if this hunk of diamond fits your finger.'

Bella's hands trembled as he slid the ring onto her finger. She laughed through her tears.

Leo chuckled, wrapping his arms around her as they lay back on the blanket, the sun warm against their skin. Bella held her hand up, watching as the diamond caught the light.

'I love you, Leo,' she whispered. 'I'll be proud to be your wife. This ring… it's perfect. It really suits my hand, doesn't it?'

Velvet Glow wandered closer, sniffing around the basket, with Danger Man not far behind.

'Why are they sniffing around the basket?' Bella asked, glancing at Leo. He grinned.

'Have a look.'

Curious, Bella propped herself up on her elbows and pulled the basket closer. Lifting the lid, she peered inside then bolted upright with a startled laugh.

'Apples!' she exclaimed, her voice ringing out in delight. She scrambled to her feet, still grinning, and reached into the basket, pulling out two rosy, ripe apples. The horses, undeterred by her sudden movement, stretched their necks closer, ears pricked forward in anticipation.

'You two don't waste any time, do you?' Bella teased as she moved toward them. She held out an apple to each horse, their soft muzzles brushing her hands as they eagerly took their treat. Their munching filled the quiet air, adding to the charm of the moment.

Leo laughed loudly, watching the scene unfold. He poured the champagne and held out a glass to her. 'To surprises,' he said, standing up next to Bella. Bella turned back to him, her eyes shining. 'To the best kind of surprises,' she agreed, clinking her glass against his as the bubbles caught the sunlight.

'To us,' Bella echoed, her heart brimming. 'And thank you, Danger Man and Velvet Glow, for bringing us together.'

She nestled into Leo's arms. The warm sun, the soft breath of the horses, and the sparkle of her beautiful engagement ring weaving a memory she knew she'd cherish forever.

Meet Dee Gibson

Dee Gibson is an Australian Author who has written in the field of Numerology, Spirituality, and Children's books.

Dee lives on the beautiful Bellarine Peninsular, in Victoria, Australia.

If you have enjoyed any of my books it would make this new author very happy, if you could spare a minute to write a short review.

Happy Reading

Dee.

www.deegibson.com.au

hello@deegibson.com.au

FB: Dee Gibson

IG DeeDeeGibson

Tik Tok DeedeeGibson

Dee Gibson is an Australian Author who has written in the field of Numerology, Spirituality, and Children's books.

Novels

Falling for Mr Love
Falling for the Trainer (release date 2025)
Falling for the Cook (release date 2025)
Forged Karma (release date 2025)

FALLING FOR MR LOVE - BOOK 1

Elsie and Bella Series Book 1

Hold onto your hats. If you want a laugh and some spontaneous interaction jump aboard and have a read, of this Fun, Flirty, romance.

Elsie and best friend Bella roll into Flemington Racecourse, bringing a dash of eccentricity and a whole lot of flair to the Melbourne Cup festivities.

Elsie and Bella are neighbours who are changing lanes in life, downsizing, to a Life Style Village.

Elsie's larger-than-life personality creates mischief wherever she goes. She's like a tornado in a meditation room.

Elsie terrorises the inmates, with her tall stories, and unwelcome quips.

Are Elsie and Bella searching for love? Have they been in jail?

Should the other wives be worried?

Definitely.

FROM AUTHOR DEE GIBSON.

FALLING FOR THE
TRAINER - BOOK 2

Elsie and Bella Series Book 2

When city girl Bella stumbles into the rural world of horse racing, she finds herself smitten with a ruggedly handsome trainer, Leo.

After a clumsy encounter involving a forbidden apple and a Melbourne Cup-winning stallion, Bella's accidental blunder sparks more than embarrassment.

Should Bella accept an invitation to a party at Leo's stud farm?

Amidst the humour, awkward encounters, and unexpected visits from an ex-wife, they realise that in the world of horse racing, no one can predict the winner.

Who will cross the finish line first? Bella, Leo, or the ex-wife.

FROM AUTHOR DEE GIBSON

FALLING FOR THE COOK

Elsie and Bella Series Book 3

WHEN HIS COWORKERS surprise him with a vacation, Justin, known simply as *Cook* leaves behind his quiet life as a stud farm chef and finds himself scuba diving on the stunning Great Barrier Reef. But when wealthy fitness mogul

Kate vanishes, Justin uncovers a chilling plot: someone wants her fortune, and they're willing to kill for it.

Thrust into danger, Justin must dive deeper than ever before, to save Kate and confront his own fears. With her air running low and killers closing in, he whisks her to safety with the help of the police and a light plane.

As they hide out on Tasmania's Cradle Mountain, passion blooms. With a bitter breakup, an attempted murder, and a deadly game unfolding around them, Justin must decide return to the safety of solitude or risk everything for true love.

Will his instincts be enough to keep Kate alive, or will their chance at love be lost forever?

'In a sea of uncertainty, love is the anchor.'

FROM AUTHOR DEE GIBSON

FALLING FOR MR WRONG - BOOK 4

Elsie and Bella Series Book 4

Emma had given up on men. Until the party where she met Todd. There he was asking her to dance, handsome as a movie star, confident and smiling. Wow! What a hunk.

He was everything she'd dreamed of a charming man with movie star looks. He was irresistible. His charisma made her feel like she was the centre of his universe.

Together, they built a family life, full of promise and joy. Emma thought she'd nailed love the second time around.

Everything changed the day Emma drove to the airport.

Then she found the 'Tiffany Tin.'

Who knew that a fake smile, a glass of wine, and some Bolognese sauce could bring truth to the surface.

Falling for Mr. Wrong is a sharp, smart, hilarious tale of betrayal, resilience, and a strong woman who won't be fooled twice.

FROM AUTHOR DEE GIBSON

FORGED KARMA

Forged Karma; released date June 2025

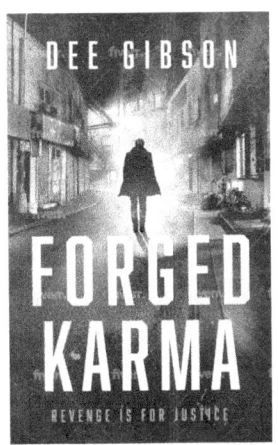

DETECTIVE CARUTHERS SOLVES CASES. He is not happy that a new recruit has been assigned to work with him on a complex murder case. This investigation has long tentacles, from Melbourne Australia, to the Cayman Islands.

To solve this murder, one person must give up every part of his life to bring the killer to justice.

Revenge isn't just for lovers.

Revenge is for Justice.

FROM AUTHOR DEE GIBSON

COPYRIGHT 2022

www.ingramcontent.com/pod-product-compliance
Lightning Source LLC
Chambersburg PA
CBHW071627140626
46555CB00021B/901